Harry Mazer

SCHOLASTIC INC.

New York   Toronto   London   Auckland   Sydney
Mexico City   New Delhi   Hong Kong   Buenos Aires

No part of this publication may be reproduced, stored in a retrieval
system, or transmitted in any form or by any means, electronic,
mechanical, photocopying, recording, or otherwise, without written
permission of the publisher. For information regarding permission,
write to Simon & Schuster Books for Young Readers,
Simon & Schuster Children's Publishing Division,
1230 Avenue of the Americas, New York, NY 10020.

ISBN 0-439-70224-0

12 11 10 9 8 7 6 5 4 3 2   4 5 6 7 8 9/0

Printed in the U.S.A.   40

First Scholastic printing, October 2004

Book design by Debra Sfetsios
The text for this book is set in Jansen Text.

ACKNOWLEDGMENTS

For their generous help as I researched this book, my grateful thanks to Jenny Akina, Emily Alina, Wendy Costa, and Pam Muñoz Ryan, and special thanks to Nori Masuda, who unstintingly gave me his time and patiently answered all my questions about the internment.

May such injustice and humiliation never recur.

—FROM A MEMORIAL PLAQUE AT THE
FRESNO COUNTY FAIRGROUNDS

1

I was walking down the middle of the road when I saw a couple of people pushing a car up a hill. There was never a lot of traffic, not with gas rationing. The man on the driver's side had one hand on the steering wheel.

"Help us out," the man said. He had on a greasy cap, and his front bottom teeth were missing.

A girl was behind the car, her shoulder against the spare tire like she had the whole weight of the car on her. She made room for me, and we pushed together. I recognized her from the school bus stop. She was that tall older girl who always had her nose in a book.

"Hi," I said. "I know you. You take the bus to school."

She looked at me through a tangle of hair and nodded.

"Push, Nance," the man said.

"I am pushing, Woody!"

"Good girl."

She muttered something girls don't say. I'd never known a girl who said things like that.

"You two kids, push the heck out of it," Woody said. "We're almost to the junkyard."

"Why don't we just push it in the ditch?" Nancy said.

"Oh, don't say that, Nance. I just paid twenty-five bucks for this baby. I love this car."

"That's about all you love," she muttered.

I was trying to figure out who he was. Not her father. You didn't talk to your father like that. Maybe an uncle or a cousin.

We finally reached the top of the rise, and the weight of the car eased. It started rolling, and Woody jumped in behind the wheel. "In like Flynn!" he yelled. "Keep pushing, kids. Faster, faster!"

The girl and I were running and pushing. "Start it," she cried. "Start it, Woody!"

The car coughed, belched black smoke, coughed again, and off it went. "Bakersfield Express," Woody yelled, sticking his head out the window.

We were left standing there in the exhaust. "Pushing this car to the junkyard—it's a joke, right?" I said to her.

"No, he practically lives in that junkyard." She brushed the hair out of her face. "This isn't the first time I've pushed his stupid car."

At the dairy on River Road I stopped. "I live over there," I said, pointing to the house across the road. "We live upstairs. Second floor."

"Uh-huh," she said, turning down the path to the river.

I watched her for a moment, then called after her, "I'm Adam!"

She raised her arm, fingers sort of waving good-bye to me.

2

My father was at Pearl Harbor when the Japanese attacked on December 7, 1941, and World War II started for America. He was an officer on the USS *Arizona*, Lt. Emory J. Pelko, and he was onboard his ship that Sunday morning.

I was there too. No, not on the ship, in the harbor. Davi Mori, Martin Kahahawai, and I had gone fishing early that morning. We had found a rowboat, and we were out on the water fooling around when we heard the drone of the planes coming over. We thought it was a practice, a navy exercise, a war game, till the bombs started falling and the boat we were in tipped and the air exploded, and we were thrown into the water.

I saw my father's ship, that great battleship the USS *Arizona*, explode and sink. There were a thousand men onboard, and most of them went down with the ship. Their bodies are still down there in the wreckage. My father, too.

I know he's gone, I know I'm never going to see him, but sometimes I can't help thinking he got free somehow and he's going to come home.

3

Right after Pearl Harbor my mother, my sister, and I were evacuated from Hawaii and sent back to the States. For a while we lived in San Diego in navy housing near the base—a couple of cheesy rooms, with a sink and a stove along one wall. I hated it there—the sunny San Diego sky was too much like the sunny Hawaiian sky, too much like the Pearl Harbor sky. I wanted to move, and I didn't care where we went.

When Mom got a letter from my grandfather Pelko, who lived all the way across the country on a farm in Adams Center, New York, I was ready to go. Mom read the letter aloud to me and Bea at supper.

Dear Marilyn,

How are you and the children? It's still winter here, and it snows every day. So much snow. It covers the windows up to the second story. I take care of the animals. I feed the fire. Every day the same thing. Every day the woodpile gets smaller and every day I think of my son, Emory. I'm an old man and it makes me sad. I hope you and the children are comfortable and warm. Perhaps in the spring you will come.

> *Sincerely yours,*
> *Oskar Pelko*

"Grandpa Pelko is Daddy's daddy," Bea said.

"You're right," I said.

"I do feel sorry for Oskar, all alone there," Mom said. "Not that he hasn't been alone for years, but now . . ." Her voice drifted off. She lit a cigarette and sat there, not eating, looking out the window. She put food out for me and Bea, but she never ate anything herself. She'd just sit with us at the table, smoking. Cigarettes and coffee—that was her food. One cigarette stubbed out and another one lit.

"Let's go live on the farm with Grandpa," I said.

"I want to live on that farm," Bea agreed.

"No, you don't," Mom said. "Winters, all that snow and cold? Uh-uh, I can't do that."

Snow sounded good to me. Anything was better than staying here, always seeing men in navy whites. Everywhere I turned, I thought I saw my father. I would catch a glimpse of an officer and my heart would start hammering, and I'd run after him. It was never my father.

"Mom, I want to move," I said. "I really want to move." I drummed my fingers on the table. "I really want to get out of here."

She put her hand over mine. "I do too, Adam, but . . ."

She puffed on her cigarette. "I don't know . . . I just can't think about it now."

"If Dad was here . . ."

Mom shot me a warning look. We had never told Bea that Dad was dead. I didn't have to say it anyway. It was like the words were printed in the air. *If Dad was here, he'd tell us where to go, he'd tell us what to do.* If he were here, he'd make Mom stop smoking so much. He'd make her eat meals. He had taken care of her. He had taken care of all of us.

"Where is Daddy?" Bea asked suddenly. She smoothed her dress. "This is my favorite dress I'm wearing, you know. I'll wear it when Daddy comes home. When is he coming home?" She sighed, like a little grown-up, like Mom sighed when she started thinking about Dad. "Oh, I know," Bea said. "He comes home when the war ends, right, Mommy?"

Mom jumped up. "The carrots are burning!" She pulled the pot off the stove and put it under the water. "Why am I always doing that?" She stared into the sink, as if there were answers there for her. "We need to look ahead. We need . . . we need to . . . to move ahead." She mashed out her cigarette and sat down again at the table.

"You okay, Mom?"

She looked at me, then handed Bea her fork. "Come on, kids, eat your food."

"You too, Mom," I said.

She took a bite of hamburger. "My cousin Shirley in Bakersfield wants us to come there."

"Bakersfield sounds good," I said. "Where's that?"

"Between here and San Francisco." Mom folded Grandpa's letter back into the envelope. "Maybe we will go," she said. "I always liked Shirley."

I put my arm around her shoulders. "Write her tonight, Mom."

"Maybe I will," she said.

4

Just before we moved to Bakersfield, I got a letter from my best friend in Honolulu.

Dear Adam,

How in heck are you? This is your friend Davi Mori from Honolulu, in case you forgot. I can't believe you went off without saying good-bye. Only one stinky postcard with your APO. I keep expecting to see your ugly mug in school. I went up around your house. I thought I'd see you. Your old neighbors saw this dangerous Jap, *and they called the cops on me. It's still crazy around here.*

You know the FBI men came to our house and took my father away and put him on Sand Island? The Sand Island Country Club. Very popular with the Japanese. Very funny. You think so? My uncle Lucas and my cousins had to pull their boat out of the water. They can't fish anymore. The FBI won't let them, they think they're going to meet up with enemy submarines.

My brother-in-law, Sam, comes to the house every day. He talks to my mom and tells her not to worry. He says we can't allow ourselves to feel guilty. We've done nothing. We are loyal Americans. He can't figure out about Pop either. The other ones that are locked up are all big in the community—Mr. Hashimi, who's the minister, and a newspaper editor and a couple of teachers from the Japanese school. What's my pop there for? He collects junk and fixes things. They don't let us see him. My mom brings food and she has to leave it at the gate.

My father's no spy. He was born in Japan, that's his problem. The Big Shots are afraid of anyone who looks Japanese, like half the people in Hawaii. Thanks a lot, Emperor Hirohito. You fixed us good. Sorry for being so gloomy. Wish you were here. How are you doing? How do you like it where you are now? When are you going to write me, you dog?

Your friend,
Davi

I put the letter away to answer once we'd moved up to Bakersfield, and then I forgot about it.

5

The apartment in Bakersfield that my mother's cousin Shirley found for us was on River Road in a big old rambling house with porches and turrets. The whole house had been broken up into apartments. The one we were renting was bigger than the apartment in San Diego, but it was still only two rooms, and the bathroom was in the hall.

"You've got to share it with the other apartments on that floor," Shirley said. She was sort of round and tiny. She didn't look anything like Mom.

"Share?" my mother said.

"Yes, honey. There's a war on now," Shirley said, as if we had to be reminded.

The door to the attic was opposite our apartment, and Mr. Medina, the landlord, said we could use it. It was a mess, filled with junk and broken-down furniture, but I moved things around. "This is going to be my room," I said to Mom, and she said okay.

I pulled a big old armoire around to make a wall and put my bed near the window. I rescued a bureau with three good drawers and found a radio, an RCA floor model, under one of the rafters. Some of the tubes in back didn't light, but I could change them.

From the window I saw the river in the distance, flashing through the trees, and I remembered Davi, Martin, and me on the water that morning, the water so peaceful we could have been floating on air. Then the bugles sounded and the flags went up on all the battleships, and we stopped rowing and just drifted.

I knew my father was onboard the *Arizona*, and I remember thinking he might be out on the deck and he'd see me in the rowboat, and he'd be mad because I wasn't supposed to be with Davi.

And then the planes came.

What if my father saw me and tried to warn me and didn't save himself? I didn't know. I would never know, and when I tried to think about it, I just went blank.

6

A week after I started school, Mr. Leesum, the principal, called me into his office. "Sit down, Adam," he said, closing his door and sitting down behind his desk. "Well." He rubbed his eyes with his forefingers. "How are you doing, Adam? How is it going?"

"Good. Fine, sir."

"I see from your records your father is missing in action?"

"No, sir, not missing. He died at Pearl Harbor."

"Died? That's awful. I'm sorry. I tried to get in the military, but they turned me down." He rubbed his eyes again. "I'm working nights in a war plant, but it's not the same thing."

There were only two other men in the whole school. The other male teachers were all in the military. Mr. Ewing, the history teacher, walked with a limp, so he was deferred, and Mr. Herrick, the English teacher, was too old.

Mr. Leesum straightened a framed picture on his desk. "Your father was at Pearl Harbor when the Japs sneak-attacked us?"

"Yes, sir. I was too."

"How's that?"

"It was sort of an accident. I was with my friends that morning, we were fishing at Pearl, and we found . . ." I stopped. I didn't want to go into the rowboat and all of that, but Mr. Leesum was leaning forward and he kept asking me questions. I ended up telling him about being out on the water, and the planes coming, and getting strafed, and my father's ship sinking.

Mr. Leesum sat back and sighed. "A terrible tragedy. So many men gone. . . ."

I didn't say anything.

"Your father died a hero's death, Adam."

"Yes, sir." My eyes stung. I pressed my lips together. I didn't want to cry in front of him. I crossed my arms over my chest and looked up at the ceiling. *Don't cry, don't cry.* Mom could cry, she was a girl, and girls cried. Not boys. Not me. My father would be ashamed of me if I cried.

I didn't cry.

7

"I'm going now, Adam," Mom said, coming up the attic stairs. She had found a job in a machine shop that made airplane parts for the navy, and she left for work in the morning just as I was getting up. It was really strange to see her in coveralls instead of dresses, her hair hidden by a kerchief.

"You're not going to fall asleep again?" she said.

"Yes, Mom," I said, jumping out of bed. Then, because she still looked anxious, I recited my morning orders. "Wake up Bea, comb her hair, make sure she eats a good breakfast and brushes her teeth, get her ready for Mrs. Henson, and have her outside by—"

"Okay, okay," she said, smiling. "My ride's here. See you later, honey."

Once I was dressed, I got Bea up. Combing her hair was the big chore. "Don't be so rough," she said, pushing my hand away.

"I'm not rough," I said, starting to brush again. "Your hair's a big mess."

We were in my room, and while I combed her hair, she

played with a doll I'd found for her on top of the armoire. It had only one arm, but a perfect porcelain head.

"You are rough, Adam."

"You want to do it yourself?"

"I caaan't."

"Stop whining."

"I'm not whiiinning."

"You don't hear yourself, do you?"

"Shut up."

"Is that the way for a young lady to talk?"

"Double shut up."

"Listen to the little lady."

"Triple shut up, Adam!" She jumped up and started opening the bureau drawers. "Ten times shut up," she shouted. She pulled out Davi's letter from the back of the drawer. "I've got your letter," she sang. "Got your letter, letter, letter. Do you have a girlfriend?"

"Yes, and her name's Bea."

"No! Truly, Adam."

"Truly, Bea. Give me that letter. It's from my friend Davi in Hawaii."

She held the letter to her nose and sniffed. "This letter smells like Hawaii. Where Daddy is. Hawaii makes me sad. I want to cry."

"Come on, let me finish your hair. Then we'll go eat cornflakes."

She sat there holding Davi's letter to her nose while I made her two ponytails and tied them off with rubber bands.

When we went outside, Mrs. Henson was waiting on the porch. "Don't you look cute, honey." She took Bea's hand and they walked off toward her house.

It was still early. Across the road a close knot of kids were waiting for the bus. I straightened the white navy cap I wore every day. It had been my father's when he was a midshipman. I still wasn't as big as him, but my head size was the same. I walked back and forth along the road, clicking my father's Zippo lighter, the one with the Navy Seal on it.

I didn't really know any of these bus kids yet. There were some kids I talked to in school, but mostly I kept to myself. I'd been to so many schools I could make friends with my eyes shut and both hands tied behind my back, but the guys here, they were so ignorant. I had heard them talking about the war, boasting about what they were going to do when they got in, all the Japs they were going to mow down, like it was easy as swatting flies.

That girl Nancy, the one I'd pushed the car with, was coming up the path from the river, her arms full of books. I thought she saw me, and I crossed over the road, expecting her to say something about us pushing the car together. She sort of nodded, but she didn't say anything, so I went back to my side of the road.

Then she crossed over and circled around me like she was taking a closer look, but she still didn't say anything. Just went around me and back across the road. Maybe it was a game. If it was, I didn't get it. What was I supposed to do? Go across now and circle around her?

On the bus she sat in back. I sat up front behind the driver, watching the road over his shoulder but thinking I should have gone in back and sat down next to her. Or anyway, said something to her. Maybe she thought she was too old to talk to me. She was a junior. Still, she could at least have said hello.

8

"*Le chapeau*, Monsieur Pelko," Mrs. Rubero said.

I took off my hat and started toward my seat in the back of the room. There was a foot on the seat. Babe Gribble's foot. He was a big, hefty guy, like my friend Martin Kahahawai. The difference was that Martin Kahahawai was calm and patient and had a sense of humor—he was everything that Babe Gribble wasn't.

Babe was sprawled back, watching me, not moving his foot, as if the seat belonged to him.

I wanted to punch him in the face. I stood there looking at the foot.

"Monsieur Pelko?"

"*Oui*, Madame Rubero." I brushed Babe's foot off the seat and sat down. I never looked at him again, but for the rest of the period I was aware of his foot in the aisle.

Every day in French class Babe Gribble had his foot on my seat. Every day I knocked it off. On Friday when I walked out of school, I saw some kids playing ball on the baseball diamond, and I went over to watch. Babe Gribble was hitting the ball out to a couple of younger kids.

He spotted me right away. "What are you doing hanging around?" he asked.

"It's a free country, remember."

I'd been about to leave, but now I just stood there and watched. He was hitting the ball pretty good, and the kids had to cover the whole field. One of them, a skinny kid wearing a red jersey, looked a lot younger than the other one. He was having trouble getting to the ball, then lobbing it in, and Babe Gribble was all over him.

"Move, you baboon," he yelled. "Throw it here!"

Nothing the kid did satisfied Babe. He was really trying, but Babe never let up on him. "You call that a throw? My little sister throws better than that." Then he turned to me and said, "Why don't you get out there in the field, Pesko? That kid's useless."

"Pelko," I said.

"Yeah, yeah, Pelko. Get your butt out there."

"Forget it." I wasn't going to do anything that he wanted me to do. "I haven't got a glove anyway," I said.

"What have you got, an alibi for everything? You got hands, meathead."

I walked away.

He squawked and made like a bird. "Chicken!"

That was it. I tucked my navy cap under my belt and trotted out to the field. I got between the two kids. Babe hit the ball high over my head. I went back and caught it and whipped it into him as hard as I could.

The kid he'd been riding got the next ball, and then I got

another one. With the three of us out there, we were getting every ball. "Let's go, Gribble," I called. "Come on, Babe Ruth, hit it. We're falling asleep out here. Let's see you hit a ball past us."

Maybe he really thought he was Babe Ruth. He was trying so hard to hit the ball past us that he missed it completely.

"You want a bigger ball, Gribble? I got a basketball here for you."

I stayed until the game broke up.

Walking home, I looked for gum wrappers and cigarette packs to bring Bea. She stripped out the inner foil for the aluminum ball she was making for the war effort. The other day I'd picked up a rubber monkey lying in a ditch at the side of the road. Some kid must have dropped it out of a car. I gave it to Bea, and she put it on the shelf next to her silver ball.

I was cutting across a field when I spotted a tiny baby rabbit. It saw me, but it just sat there, didn't even know enough to run away. I picked it up and closed my hand around it. It was warm, and I could feel it breathing. I tucked it in my pocket.

"Wait till you see what I brought you," I said to Bea when I got her at Mrs. Henson's. "A baby rabbit."

She grabbed her hair. "Will it get me?"

"Baby rabbits are nice, Bea." I took it out of my pocket. It lay in my hand without moving. I prodded it a little.

"It's dead," Bea said. "Isn't it dead, Adam? Like Daddy."

That stopped me. All this time both Mom and I had thought Bea believed us when we told her Dad was away at sea, just as he'd been away so many other times.

"Let's get a box for the rabbit," I said.

We put it into an empty cereal box and buried it under a rosebush. "Poor little baby rabbit," Bea said. "When will it come back, Adam?"

I took her hand as we walked around the side of the house. She'd figured out that Dad had died, but did she really know what that meant? Not if she thought the rabbit was going to come back.

"Bea . . . ," I started, but I didn't know what to say, what to tell her, so I didn't say anything. Why did she have to know, anyway? Let her find out when she was a little older.

9

On Monday, Babe was waiting for me after school. "Hey," he called. "Yeah, you, Pisko."

"Pelko," I said.

"Where you from, Pelko?"

I pointed to the sun in the western sky, meaning Hawaii.

"Oh, he's from heaven." A kid, his hair slicked back, snickered.

"And he's from the navy," Babe said, snapping his fingers at my cap. "Is that right, Pisko?"

"Are you asking me? You seem to know everything. Talk to my cap," I said. "This cap knows more than all you guys put together. This cap was at Pearl Harbor."

"Yeah, Mr. Big Shot. You and them Japs."

I should have shut up at that point and walked away, but I didn't. "I was there," I said. "You can believe it or not."

"You're lying." Babe was trying to look right through me with those X-ray eyes. "A kid wouldn't—they wouldn't let a kid near Pearl Harbor in a million years."

"I saw them, their planes, their bombs, our ships blowing up. It was real. Realer than this"—I swung my arms—"this *place.*" I was too excited, talking too fast. I couldn't find the words to express my disgust. "What I'm telling you is real. You know what real is? You know what war is? You think it's like the movies?"

"You're a Jap." One of Babe's pals pointed his finger at me. "Rat-tat-tat-tat. You're dead." Then they were all doing it, *rat-tat-tat-tat*, and laughing.

I walked away. I'd been too loud, said too much, gotten too mad. What did I care what they thought? My father would never have lost control that way.

I was still talking to myself when I got home. Mr. Medina was waiting for me in his black pickup truck. As soon as I saw him, I knew I was late. I was supposed to be here half an hour ago.

"About time," he said. "You ready to work or not? If I had anybody else, I wouldn't use you."

He sounded just like Babe Gribble—mean and bullying. I had been doing odd jobs for him around the house, getting twenty-five cents an hour. Mostly I pushed the lawn mower, but I'd helped him with other things too, like bringing out the garbage cans and steadying the forty-foot ladder against the house so he could clean the gutters.

Today he'd come with clippers and gloves, and he put me to work on the thorny bushes in back of the house. Those bushes were mean; they fought back. I clipped, and they scratched. I made believe it was Babe I was clipping. That made the work go faster. *Clip. Clip. Clip.* When I was done, I was sweaty, scratched up, and itchy all over.

I walked over to Mr. Medina's dairy store across the road, thinking that those bushes were definitely a fifty-cents-an-hour job. But all Mr. Medina said was, "Did you get them all?" Then he gave me the usual two dimes and a nickel.

"I think it's worth more," I blurted. I don't know where I got the nerve, but I didn't want him to think he could give me anything and I'd take it.

"Two bits is what I pay for this kind of work."

"I want real work, then."

"What do you think you've been doing?"

"I mean for fifty cents an hour."

"Fifty cents an hour! Who do you think you are? That's a man's pay."

"I can do anything you want done," I said.

"You can't drive."

"I can. My father taught me. I just don't have a license."

He looked me over, then shrugged. "My helper got drafted. I'm looking for someone in the dairy. Can you be here at four thirty every morning?"

"Every day?"

"Do cows give milk every day?"

"Yes, sir."

"Then, we have to get it every day." He showed me where they bottled the milk in back of the store. "Four thirty sharp tomorrow morning. Show up and you have a fifty-cents-an-hour job. Sundays off."

"I'll be here," I said.

*   *   *

I told Mom about the job. I thought she'd be glad, but the first thing she said was, "You won't get enough sleep, Adam. And what about school? I don't see you working and keeping up with your schoolwork the way you should."

"I'll go to bed early, Mom."

"You've got an answer for everything," she said.

"Come on, Mom, you know it's a good idea. We can use the money." I took her hand. "I don't want you to be working all the time. Fifty cents an hour, that's a man's wages."

"You're not a man yet, Adam. You're still a boy."

"Mom!" I jumped up and went to the sink. I filled a glass and gulped it down. "I gave my word to Mr. Medina. You know what Dad would say. I can't back down on my word."

"All right," she said after a moment, "but if you fall behind in your schoolwork, that's it."

The next morning Mr. Medina put me to work loading empty milk cans into the back of the truck. Then we drove out into the country. He stopped at a farm. Full milk cans were standing on a wooden platform by the road. He backed the truck up to the platform, and I jumped out, loaded the full cans into the truck, and replaced them with empties.

We stopped at six farms, and at each one I lifted the full cans and swung them onto the truck. They must have weighed more than fifty pounds each. I thought I was doing pretty good.

"You work like that," Mr. Medina said, "and you're going to wear your back out before you're old enough to vote. Don't lift. Tip the cans and roll them on. It's a lot easier, right?"

Back at the dairy he had me empty the milk cans into a stainless steel pasteurizing tank, then wash the empties. I was home just in time. Mom was waiting for me outside, and a minute later her ride came.

A bunch of women were crowded into the car. "Is that your boyfriend?" a big, curly-haired woman said, and they all laughed.

I started blushing. Mom put her arm around me. "My son was up early this morning to go to work. He was working this morning while you were still asleep, Flo."

"Her, sleep?" the woman driving the car said, and there was more laughter. "Get in, Marilyn. Let's go."

Mom got in the car and closed the door. Then she put her head out the window and called to me, "Adam, don't forget Bea."

Why did she say that? Had I ever forgotten my sister? Sometimes, these days, I didn't understand Mom. She had never worn clothes like that before or hung around with all these women or worked in a factory. My father would never have allowed it.

10

Mom, home from work, opened the refrigerator and stood there looking into it. "What should we have?"

I leaned on her shoulder. "Scrambled eggs?"

"Oh, no, honey, that's breakfast food." She shut the refrigerator. "Tell you what, we're eating out tonight. Flo told me about this great Italian place downtown called the Orange Grove."

"Mmm, I love oranges," Bea said.

"You're probably going to have spaghetti," I said.

"Mmm, I love spaghetti."

We took the bus into town, Bea chattering all the way. The Orange Grove was packed. In back a woman was at the piano playing "The Beer Barrel Polka." Every booth in front and almost all the tables in back were taken. We were lucky to find an empty, and we sat down, even though it hadn't been cleared from the people before us.

Mom pushed the dishes to the side and raised her hand for the waitress, who called the busboy, who turned out to be a busgirl. Who turned out to be Nancy from the bus stop.

"Hi," I said. She gave me a blank look. Was she too old, or too stuck up, to talk to me? "Adam," I said. "The car. The bus stop."

She nodded and began clearing the table, piling the dishes onto a tray she was balancing on one arm. I handed her a dish, helping her, I thought.

"Don't! That's my job." She yanked the dish out of my hand. The tray tipped, and everything—dishes, food, silverware—crashed to the floor. At the same moment the piano player stopped, and it seemed as if everyone in the place was looking our way.

"Sorry," I said. I bent down and started picking up stuff.

"Leave it alone," Nancy hissed. "Don't touch anything." Her hair was in her face. She looked crazy mad. She looked like she hated me. She didn't come near our table again.

The next morning, getting on the bus, I saw her. "Uh, hi," I said. For a moment it was the restaurant all over again. Nothing. The blank look. And then she said, "Jerk."

"Hey." I shrugged. "It was an accident. I'm sorry. Okay?" I was talking to her back. She was walking away.

Every day I saw her on the bus. I was going to say, "Hi, remember me, the jerk?" What would that get me? And why did I like her? Well, she was tall, and older, and she said things. She wasn't like any girl I had ever known. Not that I knew that many.

I saw her once in the auditorium, but I couldn't talk to her. It was a program for the junior and senior high about helping the war effort and buying war bonds, and she was playing clarinet in the band. I didn't think I'd ever get to talk to her again. But then one day I was going into the lunchroom and she was going out of the lunchroom, and I almost walked right into her. "Hey," I said. "Sorry."

"Are you always sorry?"

"Sorry," I said.

"You're impossible, Adam."

"You remembered my name!"

"No big thing," she said. "Calm down, child."

11

"Ladies and gentlemen," Mr. Ewing said one day toward the end of history class. "How many of you have family in the service?" Hands went up all over the room. "All right," he said. "Then, you all should be interested that we have a hero in our midst."

Everyone looked around. I did too. I was in back, a little sleepy from working in the dairy that morning.

"Adam Pelko, I understand you were at Pearl Harbor." Mr. Ewing limped to the pull-down map and pointed. "Here we are, and there's Pearl Harbor. Adam, please come up front and tell us in your own words about your experience."

I walked slowly to the front. What should I say? "*Hero*'s a big word," I said. "I don't think I qualify. I was just there."

"Where were you exactly?" Mr. Ewing asked.

"I was in a rowboat by French Island. We were fishing."

"Where were the battleships?"

"Right there, tied up along Ford Island. It was Sunday morning. I saw them raise the flags, and the bands were playing 'The Star-Spangled Banner,' and then the planes came. . . ."

"Go on," Mr. Ewing said.

"All I could see was fire and smoke and flags burning, everything burning, even the water was burning. And my father's ship, the *Arizona* . . ." My voice broke, and I became aware of the class. They were looking at me, their mouths open.

I stood there with my fists clenched. Then I walked out.

The halls were empty. In the bathroom I leaned over the sink, letting the water run over my face.

By noon that day the word about me had spread, and it seemed as if every boy in school wanted to talk to me. In the lunchroom they crowded around, asking questions. "You were there? December seventh? You were right there? You saw the Jap planes?"

A boy named Walter jumped up on a table and saluted. "Hey, Adam Pelko, my brother's in the navy. What you did was incredible. Were you wounded?"

I nodded.

"Where?"

I pointed to my back.

"There? Did it go all the way in? What was it, a bullet?"

"I don't know."

Out of the corner of my eye I saw Babe, not close, but listening with that disbelieving, mean look on his face.

They knocked into me in the hall. My cap went flying. Babe watched, his hands in his pockets. "Your cap's on the floor, hero."

I picked it up to a lot of chortling. "You want me to knock his lights out, Babe?" one of his pals asked.

Babe looked at me, sort of smiling. "Get you next time," he said.

Dear Adam,

I got your postcard with your new address in Bakersfield. It took two weeks to get here, which is why I'm going to send this airmail even though it's kind of expensive. I want to tell you what happened with my father, because we don't know where he is. Remember how he was arrested after Pearl Harbor and put on Sand Island? Well, he isn't there anymore. They moved him and a bunch of other men to the States, and we don't know where he is, except we think it's somewhere out west, probably in California, from what people are saying.

My mother wrote to my cousin Frank Mori in Fresno to find out about my father, but the letter came back and now we don't know what to do. My uncle Lucas wanted to go to California, but everyone told him not to. What if he goes there and they call him a spy, and he ends up in prison too?

I want to ask you a favor. Would you go to Fresno for us and find my cousin Frank Mori and give him the letter I'm enclosing? It's to my father. My cousin will get it to him. My mother says my father has to hear from us. She says he's just a family man, and he has to know that we're okay. Fresno is near where you are. I looked at the map. My cousin owns a hotel in Fresno, the Hotel Royale on J Street. Anybody there would know where that is. Sure hope you can help us out—my mom's getting pretty desperate.

Your friend,
Davi
PS: My mother says she knows you're a good person and will do it.

12

The next morning I sat down next to Nancy on the bus. I wanted to talk to her, but she was reading a book. I had Davi's letter with me, and I took it out and read it again. Going to Fresno wasn't a big deal, but when was I going to do it? I was working every morning for Mr. Medina, plus extra hours on the weekend.

Just before the bus got to school, Nancy closed her book and said, "Oh, hi," like she'd just noticed I was there.

"Hi," I said. "Good book?"

"Great book."

"What's it called?"

She held it up so I could read the title: *A Tree Grows in Brooklyn.*

"It's about trees? That doesn't sound too interesting."

"There's a tree in it, but it isn't about trees. It's about this girl, Francie, who's poor and doesn't have any money, but it doesn't stop her from doing what she wants to do."

"I see you reading all the time," I said.

"I love to read."

"Are you going to be a teacher or something?"

"Yes. I want to be an English teacher." The bus was emptying, and we stood up. "What were you reading?" she asked.

"A letter from my friend in Hawaii." I showed her the envelope. "I used to live in Honolulu." We moved toward the front of the bus. "Are you working today?"

"Not till Friday," she said.

"I work every morning."

"How come every morning?"

"Do cows give milk every day?" I said as we got off the bus. She smiled, and I told her about the job and the milk cans, and even showed her the muscle in my arm. "I bet those cans, full, weigh a hundred pounds."

"Superman!"

Afterward I was sure she was laughing at me, showing my arm that way, like a little kid. I could have kicked myself.

Sunday, Mom and Bea and I were outside on the porch. It was hot, too hot to be indoors. Bea was playing with a pink ball, and my mother, her hair still wet from the shower, was talking to Mrs. LaValley, who lived on the first floor.

"Those girls I work with are wonderful," Mom said, sitting down next to Mrs. LaValley on the glider. "They have so much on them—kids, husbands away in the service—it's all on them, and you never hear a word of complaint. I admire them so much."

"Well, I think you're wonderful too, Marilyn," Mrs. LaValley said. She had flaming red hair that I was always tempted to touch. She got up and straightened her skirt. "I didn't expect to like working so much either," she said, giving me a smile. "Imagine me, a woman, working on the railroad. A car knocker! Did you ever hear anything so ridiculous?"

"Well, I never thought I'd be running a drill press," Mom said. "Drill press! The only thing I ever pressed were shirts."

Mrs. LaValley laughed and held out her hands. "Look at those hands. I can never get all the dirt out, but when I get that pay envelope, I don't care." She gave me another smile as she went back inside.

"Mom?" I sat down next to her and told her about Davi's letter.

"You still see that boy?" she said.

"I don't see him, Mom. He's in Hawaii and I'm in California."

She pushed her feet against the floor, making the glider creak. "Don't be clever, Adam. You know what I mean."

"Okay," I said. "I'm just trying to figure out when I can go to Fresno."

"You can't go," she said.

"What?"

"I said you can't go." She gave the glider another push.

"I have to go there, Mom. Davi's my friend and he's asked me to do this. You wouldn't want me to—"

"Adam, listen to me. I don't want you to do it. I don't want you going off to Fresno by yourself into . . . into . . . I don't know what!"

"Mom, look." I tried to show her the letter again. I wanted her to see what Davi had written. What was she afraid of? "It's about his father," I said.

"Maybe you should remember your father."

"What does that mean?"

"It means he told you to be careful with the friends you make. Didn't he say that?"

"Yes, but—"

"No, no buts. He told you we were going to be fighting Japan, he told you that before the war broke out, didn't he? And he was right. And he warned you not to be friends with that Japanese boy. That's what I'm talking about. Honoring your father's memory."

I jumped up. "I do honor his memory! You shouldn't say that to me."

"Shouldn't?" my mother said.

"And he's not Japanese, Mom, he's American, the same as us. And he's got nothing to do with what happened."

"Are we sure of that, Adam? Do we really know that?"

I walked away, into the house, up the stairs. It was dark, hot, and noisy, and I smelled cabbage, a smell I hated. I went all the way up to my room, and then I came down again and out on the porch and sat down on the steps next to Bea. "Throw your ball here," I said. I didn't look at my mother.

Bea flung the ball at me. "Don't throw so hard. Like this." I tossed it underhand to her, and she caught it in her skirt. "Good. Now, you throw it to me the same way."

"Adam," my mother said. She was looking off toward the river. "I don't want you to get involved with this boy. It could be dangerous."

"It's Davi, Mom. He's just a person, like me. If it was me and I asked him to do something, he'd do it. I know he would."

She tapped a cigarette on the back of her hand. "You don't owe him anything. I'm thinking of you, Adam, that's my job. You're still a boy and you don't always have the best judgment."

I threw the ball up in the air and caught it.

"I don't want you going to Fresno. Do you hear me, Adam?"

"I hear you," I said, and I threw the ball as hard as I could, clear across the road.

13

"You ever think about living on your own?" I asked Nancy. "I've been thinking about it." I knew it was crazy, but when you want to do something, and your mother's standing in your way, and you don't agree with her, this is one of the things you think about.

We were walking home from school together. I'd asked Nancy just before we were supposed to get on the bus. I still couldn't believe she'd agreed. It was a long walk. "Want me to carry your books?" She had a huge armful.

"Why?"

"Aren't they heavy?"

"Very. Good training for living on my own, which I think about all the time, since you asked, and which is something I'm definitely going to do at some point."

"Will they let you do it?"

"Who's going to stop me? Woody? He's not my father, in case you think he is. He's my mother's annoying boyfriend. I don't have a father."

"Everyone has a father."

"Thanks for the biology lesson. It's none of your business,

but I'll tell you anyway. My father is nothing to me." She shifted her books. "All I care about is my mother."

"Sorry," I started to say, and caught myself.

"So that's the scoop on my father, and we're not talking about him anymore. What about your father?"

"My father . . ." I coughed. "He died."

"Yeah, I heard somebody say something about that. Pearl Harbor, right? And you were there? I didn't know if it was true or just some big made-up story."

"No, it's true. I got a gun and everything."

"How old are you, anyway?"

"How old do you have to be to have somebody try to kill you?"

"Really? Kill you? Okay, that's enough, don't tell me about it. I hate war stories." She took my hand. "You want to see where I live?"

I couldn't take my eyes off our hands together. I didn't say anything, just turned down the path to the river with her. I didn't care where we went. She pointed to a bunch of unpainted shacks. "The last one's ours. The one with the roof made of soda signs."

"That's . . . original," I said.

She dropped my arm. Did she think I was looking down on her for living in a place like this? But it was funny, living in a house with soda signs for a roof. "It's nice when it rains," she said. "I love the sound of rain on a tin roof."

"Must be sort of like camping." I wished she'd take my hand again.

"You wouldn't want to camp here. Or live here."

We sat down on a rock in the river. It was all sandy bottom now, just a trickle of water. I kept looking at Nancy, wondering what she would say if I tried to kiss her. She'd probably smack me in the face.

"So what's that expression on your mug mean?" she said.

"I don't know," I lied. "I'm just thinking about my friend." I pulled out Davi's letter and read it to her.

"What'd they arrest his father for?"

"For nothing."

"He must have done something, Adam. The government doesn't arrest people for nothing."

"I'm telling you, Nancy, it was the day after Pearl Harbor, and they rounded up a bunch of these Japanese men. Mr. Mori repairs bicycles. He's the nicest man." I dug a stick into the sand. "They arrested him because he was born in Japan, period."

"Well, don't get so excited. You know you can't trust them."

"I know I can trust Davi," I said. "My mother acts like going to Fresno would be disloyal to my father. Does that make sense to you?"

Nancy shrugged. "It's her point of view." We sat there in silence for a few minutes. I kept snapping sticks. Nancy stood up. "I've got to get home and start supper."

"Okay," I said. "See you."

"You going to stay here?"

"Maybe."

"Well, don't look so gloomy." She put her hand on my head. "You know what I really think? If you want to do it, you should do it, Adam. If your father knew you were doing something for your friend, he'd be proud of you, wouldn't he?"

I nodded. "I think so. I think he would."

"So do it," she said.

14

In history class Mr. Ewing was talking about the war again. He rotated the big globe of the world he kept on his desk. "You see where the German army is in Libya now?" He pointed. "The Allies are here and here."

I was only half listening. I was thinking about going to Fresno. Nancy had said, "So do it," as if it were as simple as that. Maybe it was.

"The Germans have got a crackerjack general," Mr. Ewing was saying. "Who knows his name?"

"General Rommel," I said. That was easy. I read the newspaper every morning while Bea and I were eating breakfast.

A boy came in and handed Mr. Ewing a note. "Adam," Mr. Ewing said, "they want you in the office."

I got right up. I thought of Bea. I thought of my mother. I thought something had happened. "Do you know what they want?" I asked the boy. He shook his head. I followed him down the corridor toward the office.

He stopped at the boys' room. "Hang on a sec." He opened the door, and before I knew what was happening, he pulled me in.

"Look who's here," Babe said. His boys were with him. "The hero."

I lunged for the door, but they pulled me back and pinned me against the wall.

"We just want to ask you something," Babe said. "You said you were wounded. On your back? We want to see that wound."

"Let go of me."

Someone yanked up my shirt. "Come on, big hero, let's see it. Let's see the bullet hole."

They were all talking.

"Lemme see it!"

"Anybody see a hole?"

"I see a little scratch."

"Some girl do that to you?"

"He's a liar," Babe said. "I told you guys it was all total BS. He made that whole story up. He's a fake. And his father, if he even has a father, he's a fake too."

I spit at him. I wanted to tear his mouth out. "Shut up about my father!"

They dragged me toward the toilet. "Stick his head in it."

"Flush him down."

They were laughing. Then the bell rang, and a moment later they were gone.

In Mom's room the next morning I took the crew picture of my father on the *Arizona* out of the frame and put it into my history book. It showed the whole crew, officers and men together, up on the deck under the big eight-inch guns.

On the bus I showed the picture to Nancy. She looked at it carefully. "I don't have a picture of my father," she said. "Have no idea of what he looks like. Your father is really good looking."

"I'm going to show this to Babe." I told her how they'd ambushed me the day before. "I don't care what he says about me, but he's going to take back what he said about my father. I'm going to make him eat his words."

"You're wasting your time, Adam," Nancy said. "I know those Gribbles. They all have their brains where they sit. Once a Gribble gets it in his head that you think you're better than him—"

"I don't think I'm better."

"Adam. You have this way of looking at people."

"What are you talking about?"

"You look at people. You're always looking at me."

"I am?"

"I am?" she mimicked. "You know you do. If you look people in the eye too much, it's not a good thing. Look a dog in the eye, and you know what he does? He goes for you. Babe's that kind of dog, Adam. My advice is to stay away from him."

I heard her, but I didn't care.

I waited for Babe in the lunchroom. I had the picture out on the table, and kids kept coming around to look at it. "Man!" Walter said. "That's your father?"

I nodded and looked around for Babe. I had it all planned out. I wasn't going to say anything at first, just call him over, point to the picture, to the ship, and then to my father. I waited, but Babe never showed up. When I finally saw him, later that afternoon, I caught him by surprise. It was on the stairs between classes, and for once he was alone.

"I have something to show you." I took the picture out of my book and pushed it in his face.

"Out of my way," he barked.

"See that ship?" I said. "That's the USS *Arizona*. See the crew? See the officers? There—right there, that's my father." My voice was shaking, but I didn't care. "That's him there, in his uniform. Lieutenant Emory Pelko of the United States Navy."

Babe snatched the picture out of my hand. "So what?" he said, and he dropped it.

"Hey!" I snatched up the picture and chased down the stairs after him. I was going to kill him.

I caught him and shoved him against the wall. "Say you were wrong about my father. Say you're sorry. Say it!"

He punched me, and for a moment we were fighting. Then he got away from me and ran.

"You're a coward," I yelled, going after him.

"He didn't say another word," I told Nancy later. "He ducked into a room and hid behind the teacher."

"He knew he was wrong," she said.

"He couldn't even look me in the eye."

It was good to talk to Nancy about it. And when I wrote to Davi, I'd tell him about Babe. I hadn't answered his letter yet because I still didn't know when I'd be able to go to Fresno.

15

"Adam! Adam!"

I was in back of the dairy Saturday morning, cleaning the stainless steel tanks and pipes, when I heard Nancy calling me. I dropped the hose and clumped outside in Mr. Medina's rubber boots.

"I've got you a ride to Fresno," she said. "Woody's going to Oakland tomorrow morning, and he said he'd take you there."

"Tomorrow morning? I have to talk to my mother."

That got me a raised eyebrow. "Adam, it's a free ride. No money. The right day. Sunday's your day off, isn't it? Sometimes you just have to grab things. What do I tell Woody, yes or no?"

"Okay, yes," I said. I didn't want her to think I couldn't make up my own mind.

The next morning I went down the stairs at five o'clock, holding my shoes and a bag with a couple of peanut butter sandwiches, hoping my mother didn't wake up. I told myself again that she didn't have to know what I was going to do. She'd think I'd gone in to work today. I'd be to Fresno and back before she even knew it.

Outside it had started getting light, but a gray mist hung over everything. When Woody's car came bumping up from the river, I got right in, but I didn't really relax till we were out on the highway.

"Good old Route Ninety-nine," Woody said, and he banged the wheel. He was wearing a short-sleeved shirt, and where he'd had a gap in his mouth, there were teeth now. He drove with his arm out the window. I looked at his thick arms and then at mine. I had a ways to go.

"So you're a friend of Nancy's?" Woody asked.

I nodded. Didn't he remember that I'd helped push his car, *this* car? It didn't matter, it was good being in the car, on the road, rolling along. Anything could happen. Up ahead or around the next bend I might see something I'd never seen before.

"Got a light, chief?" Woody had an unlit cigarette between his teeth.

I pulled out my father's Zippo lighter and held it to his cigarette.

"That thing is a blowtorch," Woody said. "Want a drag?"

I took a puff, then handed it back.

"I'm gonna get me a defense job in Oakland," Woody sang off-key, "and make me some real mon-ee."

"And maybe join the nav-ee," I chimed in.

"Are you out of your mind, chief? I'm going to build ships, not get sunk in one. Why would I want to get myself killed when I can be making money?"

"What about the war?" I asked.

"I just hope it lasts another year so I can make some real cash."

I sat back, my eyes half closed, and watched the road. We were rolling along, the green a blur, but I wanted to go faster, fast enough to crack out of this world, like breaking out of an egg, and there, on the side of the road, would be a man, and it would be my father, and he'd say, "Where have you been, Adam? I've been waiting for you."

"Nuts," Woody said. "We got a flat." He bumped the car off the road. "Okay, let's go, we got a little work here."

I helped him jack up the car and put on the spare. Then we drove to a garage to get the tube repaired, only it was so full of patches it was hopeless, and he had to buy a new tube.

"I don't have the money for that," Woody said, kicking the tube across the floor. "What've you got on you, chief?"

There went my free ride.

When we were on the road again, Woody started grousing about, well, everything. Gas rationing. Food rationing. Cars. The army. "You can't buy a tire with treads anymore . . . the army takes everything . . . how's a man supposed to go to work . . . coupons for everything . . . I'm—"

He was interrupted by another flat, a blowout, and this time the tire was ruined. We jacked up the car again and the spare went back on, and we drove to the nearest garage. The same thing all over, except this time he had to buy a whole new tire. Well, not new. Used.

"What have you got for me, chief?" Woody asked.

I didn't want to give him the rest of my money. I gave him four singles and kept three. The "new" tire had a flat spot, but Woody didn't notice until we were rolling and the car started bumping again. After he cursed the garage and the garage owner and the military, Woody's solution was to go faster, and then even faster. The car bounced along like a kangaroo. Everything was shaking, but Woody kept accelerating.

"It's going to smooth out," he said. That was when the wheel fell off—I saw it rolling along next to us—and for a second everything did smooth out. Then the car hit the pavement, metal on stone, scraping, screeching, sparks flying.

We jumped out and watched the car slide over the embankment, down an incline, and into a tree. Woody ran down and pulled his suitcase out of the backseat. The car was smoking and then burning. For once Woody didn't say a word, just stood there with his fingers laced behind his neck, shaking his head and breathing hard.

I didn't say anything either. I was holding the bag of sandwiches so tightly my fingers cramped.

A man in a 1937 black Buick pulled over. "Anybody hurt?"

"Just my car. It's a wreck. How about a lift?" Woody said.

"You bet. I'm on my way to the Bay Area."

"You're on." Woody got in front and I got in back, and just like that we were on the road again. Woody turned and gave me a wink, like nothing had happened.

The man was a big animal veterinarian, and as he drove

he gave a lecture on delivering foals and calves.

Woody kept saying, "Is that right? You could have fooled me."

I was hoping he would drive me into Fresno, but he stopped where the road divided. "Fresno's that way," he said, and I got out.

"You take it easy now, chief," Woody said. He gave me a wink, and they drove off.

16

I sat under a tree eating one of my peanut butter sandwiches. A convoy of green military trucks passed, carrying soldiers under flapping canvas. "Hey, sailor," a soldier yelled, "where's your boat?"

My hand went to my cap. "Boats are for oars," I called.

Farm trucks loaded with produce passed, and cars and more military trucks. I started walking, my thumb out. Each time a car passed, the wind pulled at my shirt. I fingered the Zippo lighter. *Dad, I'm here for Davi. I know you don't like that, but it's just this one time. He's my friend, and I promised.* In the distance I saw a shimmer of what looked like trees and a blur of something red, and I walked faster.

GIs hitchhiking on the other side of the road were getting rides. When I didn't get one right away, I began to think that I'd never get to Fresno, never find Mr. Mori, never get home in time. I moved along, trying not to think too far ahead or how mad my mother was going to be.

A truck bounced toward me across a field and stopped at the edge of the road, and for a second I thought I had a ride.

There were two men in the cab, and one of them was motioning to me. "You. C'mere."

No ride. Just a drunk guy. I kept walking as if I hadn't heard him.

"Hey! You, Jap! I'm talking to you. I told you to c'mere."

I glanced over my shoulder. He had a gun pointed at me. I stopped.

"I got one, Warren," he said to the driver. "I said 'Jap,' and he stopped. See the way he walks, with his toes out? That's the way Japs walk, like ducks. I'm gonna blow his head off. Where'd you steal that U.S. Navy cap? Get it off your black, greasy head."

"This is my father's cap," I said. I didn't take my eyes off the gun.

"He's no Jap," the driver said. "He's just a kid, you moron. Where you going, kid? Want a ride? Come on, climb in, don't mind him. My partner here is patriotic. He's dying to kill a Jap."

"That's okay." I started moving away. "I don't need a ride." I didn't run. I didn't look back. I just kept going.

Davi hated the word *Jap*. I had always thought he made too much fuss over it. It was just a word, and everybody said it. But I'd almost been killed because of that word. And if Davi had been here, the guy would have shot him. No questions asked.

When I finally looked back, the truck was gone, but I picked up a rock anyway. Up ahead I saw what looked like a high red roof. I was more than walking now. I was running toward Fresno.

A car pulled up next to me. "Want a ride, sailor?"

I hesitated, ready to say no, but a boy was driving and a girl was sitting next to him. They looked okay. "Fresno?" I asked.

"Sure. Hop in."

I dropped the rock and opened the door. "Billy, we're not going to Fresno," the girl said as I got in back. "It's not personal," she added, turning around to me.

"Sailor, what's your expert opinion?" Billy asked. "I'm seventeen. You think I should wait to go in, until I'm drafted?" Then he answered his own question. "I'm going to volunteer."

"Mom's not going to sign for you," the girl said.

"Liz, don't be such a pill. I have to volunteer, it's the only way I'll get to be a pilot."

"Your eyes have to be twenty-twenty."

"My eyes are perfect. See that Burma-Shave sign up there? I can shoot the period right off it."

They kept at each other like that all the way to Fresno. After what had happened with those guys in the truck, it was actually kind of relaxing.

"Where do you want to be dropped, sailor?" Billy asked.

I sat up. "J Street."

"That's in Chinatown," Liz said. "What are you going there for? That's where all the Japs are."

"Were," Billy said. "They can't live in Fresno anymore. They've got them all rounded up. They had the army out and everything."

"Well, I think it's stupid," Liz said. "I go to school with Lily Nagushi, and she's okay."

"They had to do it," Billy said. "You're too trusting. Just like a girl. They could be spying, doing things against our country. Isn't that right, sailor?"

"I don't know about that spy stuff," I said. I thought of Hawaii right after Pearl Harbor, when everyone was scared and there were so many crazy rumors, like the one about Japanese spy dogs barking in Morse code.

Billy dropped me off on the corner of J Street near a movie theater. "You take it easy, pal."

"You too," I said. Then I stuck my head in the window and said, "I've got a friend, his name is Davi Mori. You'd like him. He's Japanese—I mean his parents are from Japan, but they live here now, and they'd never do anything against us. They love this country. That's why they're here."

"So what are you saying?" Billy asked.

"Well—just that not everyone who's Japanese is a spy. In fact, I bet most of them aren't."

"See," Liz said. "I told you, Billy. Like Lily Nagushi. Now, why did they take her out of school? The sailor says I'm right." They were still arguing as they drove off.

17

I went by the entrance to the Hotel Royale twice before I found the door between a clothing store and a Japanese bathhouse. Both of them were boarded up.

I looked up a dark flight of stairs and hesitated, but then I heard voices. Up on the second floor three men in undershirts were playing cards. It was a low-ceilinged room with windows looking out over the street.

"My hand, Leroyan," a man with froggy eyes said. None of them paid any attention to me.

"Wait a minute." Leroyan put his pipe down and stood up. "I quit. I can't win a hand here." He turned to me. "What do you want, kid?"

"I'm looking for Frank Mori," I said.

"No more Frank Mori." Froggy Eyes shuffled the cards. "Leroyan here, he's the big cheese now."

"I need to speak to Frank Mori, sir. Do you know where I can find him?"

"Hey," a red-faced man said. "He called you 'sir.' That's a first." He spit into a bucket.

"What do you want Mori for?" Leroyan asked.

"I have to give him a letter."

"You Western Union?"

"No, sir."

"Well, give it to me, then. I'll see that he gets it."

"I need to give it to him in person. Is he going to be gone long?"

"Come back when the war's over." They were all laughing.

"Maybe you're looking to buy something," the red-faced man said. "What do you need? Maybe your mother wants something. I've got a kitchen table and four good chairs, all kinds of pots and dishes. Tell her to come around and ask for Bill Carpenter. Everyone in Chinatown knows me."

"You don't even have to remember his name," Leroyan said. "Just ask for the biggest thief in town."

"Look who's talking," Bill Carpenter said. "Mrs. Yamamoto was happy to see me come along. What was she going to do with her piano, carry it on her back? And the table and the couch? I felt sorry for those people. They can't help being Jap. They didn't start the war. Their emperor over there in Japan started the war. She's stuck, they're all stuck. The little I could give them was appreciated, believe me. I, at least, felt some pity for them. I paid money."

"Is that why she hit you with a fry pan?" Leroyan said. "Or was it her fancy dishes she cracked over your head?"

"So what'd you give Mori for this place?"

"None of your business. I'll tell you, it cleaned me out."

"When will Mr. Mori be here?" I asked again.

"Boy, you're a pest! Mori is not connected with this hotel

anymore." Leroyan relit his pipe. "Get it through your head, kid. You don't look stupid. Listen to what I'm telling you. This is my hotel now. I am the sole proprietor."

"But I need to find Mr. Mori."

"Do you think he's still over on M Street?" Leroyan asked the other men.

"I don't know," Bill Carpenter said. "I think they're all cleaned out, but you could ask at Spino's Grocery, kid. Frank used to live right behind the store."

18

M Street looked deserted and most of the stores were closed. I saw a sign in a store window that said CHINESE HERE, and another one that said WE'RE AMERICANS. On the sidewalk in front of Spino's Grocery Store someone had chalked JAP LOVER.

A tray of yellow cakes in the store window reminded me how hungry I was. Maybe I'd buy one as soon as I found Mr. Mori. Just as Leroyan had said, there was the alleyway and, in back, a small house.

The door was open. I looked inside. It was a mess, mostly empty, just some broken stuff. "Hello?" I said. I stepped inside. "Anybody home? Mr. Mori?"

I picked up a photo of a man and two kids standing by a car. It looked like a Sunday picture, all of them dressed up for church. I thought the man was Frank Mori. He looked a little like Davi.

"Put that down!"

A woman holding a baseball bat was standing in the doorway. She snatched the photo from me. "That's not yours. Get out of here."

"Is this where Mr. Mori lives?"

"Out! Out!" she shouted. "Get out. He's not here."

"I'm not trying to do anything," I said. "The door was open, and—"

"Out," she said. "There's nothing left to steal! You should be ashamed of yourself."

"I'm not stealing. Honestly, I'm not."

She pushed me out. "Let them arrest the bad ones like you, not the good ones. Not Frank Mori!"

"Did you say they arrested Mr. Mori?"

"Yes, I said that. Where have you been, on the moon? Don't you read the newspapers? The Moris lived in this house for twelve years, them and their children, and they're all gone. Frank and Jane and the kids. Don't you know anything? Everyone of Japanese ancestry had to go. The army was here. They gave them a week to get rid of everything—business, cars, furniture—two suitcases per person, that's all they could take."

She drew a breath. "What do you want, anyway?"

"I'm supposed to give Mr. Mori this letter." She took it from me, looked at the envelope and the stamp, turned it over, looked at it again.

"My friend's mother wrote it," I said.

"All right," she said finally. "Come with me. I can think better in the store."

Inside she put the bat down behind the counter. "They didn't even let little June Mori inside the library to return her book. What did they think she was going to do? A little girl like that!"

"Where are they now?" I asked.

"They took them all to the fairgrounds." She sighed and looked around. "You want something?"

I pointed to the yellow cakes, and she gave me one, but when I tried to pay her, she wouldn't take the money. "What good are they to me? You see how many I sold? Zero. What am I going to do now? All my neighbors are gone. All my customers. Who's going to buy my groceries?"

Her eyes were red. "Who am I going to talk to? The whole neighborhood gone. They took them away to the fairgrounds like a bunch of animals."

Before I left, she wrapped some more cakes in paper and gave them to me. She walked outside with me and told me again how to get to the fairgrounds. "If you see Mrs. Mori, you tell her I miss her."

I nodded. I wanted to do something for her, and I pointed to the chalk scrawl on the sidewalk. "Do you want me to erase that? I can wash it off for you."

"No. Leave it alone," she said. "If that's the way they think, that's what I am. I'm not ashamed."

19

It was so hot that I went from tree to tree, from one patch of shade to another. At the fairgrounds I saw the horse stalls first, then the grandstands, then the barbed wire.

Soldiers were at the gate, directing traffic. "I'm looking for somebody in there," I said to one of the MPs.

"Are you family?"

"It's a friend—"

"Only family allowed inside."

"I just want to talk to him for a minute," I said.

He held up his hand to stop a car. "I told you, only family. No exceptions."

I stood there for a moment, then walked away along the fence. On the other side there were people everywhere. Frank Mori was in there somewhere. I thought of just tossing the envelope over the fence or shouting out his name. Two stupid ideas.

"Ball! Ball!" Two boys stood at the fence calling to me. "Our ball. It's there, in the ditch."

"You want me to get it?" Two stupid ideas and one stupid question. I found the ball and held it up. "Who gets it?"

"Me," the little kid said. "Throw it to me, not Mikey."

"Go ahead," Mikey said. He looked about my age. "Throw it to Ben."

I lobbed the ball over the fence, and Ben caught it neatly. "Good catch, Ben," Mikey said. "Where're you from?" he asked me.

"Bakersfield. I'm looking for—"

"I've never been to Bakersfield. What's it like?"

"It's okay. I haven't been there that long either."

"Where'd you come from before that?"

"Honolulu. My dad was based at Pearl Harbor."

Something in his face changed, tightened. "Come on, Ben," he said. "Let's go."

"Wait a second," I said. "I'm not blaming you guys for Pearl Harbor."

"Big deal," Mikey said. "Then you're the only one who isn't. How do you think we got stuck in here?"

"Hey, I'm sorry. Do you know Frank Mori?"

"We know Mr. Mori," Ben said.

"Shut up," Mikey said.

"I have to talk to him," I said.

"Let me guess, you want to buy his truck," Mikey sneered. "What are you going to give him for it, a couple of cantaloupes?"

"You want me to get him?" Ben asked.

"I told you, shut up."

"His cousin gave me a letter for him from his aunt," I said.

"How do you know Mr. Mori's cousin?" Mikey asked.

"I told you, I lived in Honolulu. Davi Mori's my best friend."

Mikey kicked the fence. "Are you bulling me?"

"Let your brother get Mr. Mori for me, okay?"

Mikey looked at me, his hands in his pockets. Then he turned to his brother. "Okay, Ben. Go get Mr. Mori. You know where to find him?"

"I know. In the kitchen."

Both of us watched Ben run off. Then we just stood there, him on one side of the fence, me on the other. "Is Ben your brother?" I asked, finally.

"One of them."

"How many have you got?"

"Five. Ben's the baby."

"I've just got one sister. Are all your brothers here?"

He shook his head. "Mark's in the army, he went in straight from ROTC in college, Billy's in Chicago in college, and Matthew's in New York City."

Ben came running back. "He's coming. I found Mr. Mori."

A moment later a man in a white shirt and tie came around the building. It was the man in the photo. "Hello, sir," I said. "Mr. Mori?"

He looked at me hard. "Do I know you?"

"No, sir. I went to your hotel to find you, and—"

"You went to my hotel." He paused. "All right, boys," he said to Ben and Mikey, "thank you." He waited until they left, then he said, "So you were at the Hotel Royale. When were you there?"

"This morning."

"And how was it? Are they busy?"

"I don't know. I saw Mr. Leroyan and a couple of other men." If Mr. Mori had been in the Hotel Royale when I came up the stairs, I thought, he wouldn't have been playing cards. He would have been standing behind the counter, checking things over.

"Ah. Leroyan. And what did Mr. Leroyan say?"

"That Mrs. Spino would know where you were. She told me to come here and to tell you, I mean Mrs. Mori, that she misses her."

Frank Mori nodded. "I'll give Mrs. Mori the message."

"The reason I came, though, is this." I passed Davi's letter through the fence. *Mission accomplished, Davi.*

Mr. Mori unfolded the letter and read it. "Well," he said, "thank you for bringing this to me, young man, but this letter is for my uncle, and unfortunately I can't deliver it." He put it back in the envelope. "I'm going to have to ask you to bring it to him. I believe he's at Manzanar."

"Mr. Mori . . ." I backed away. "I've got to go home. I don't even know where Manzanar is."

"It's not that far. Does your family live here in Fresno?"

"No, we're in Bakersfield."

"Perfect. There's a train from there that goes up through the Tehachapi Pass once a day and over to the

Owens Valley. That's where Manzanar is."

The sun was so hot. I kicked the dirt. All I could think was, *Mission* un*accomplished*.

He reached into his pocket. "I can pay you something. My uncle really needs to see this letter, to know that his family is all right."

"I don't want money," I said.

"I apologize. I understand, this is friendship."

"Yes."

"I look at you and I see a good person. I know you'll do this." He pushed the letter through the fence and—I didn't know what else to do—I took it.

20

"Adam, you idiot," I said to myself.

All the way to the train station in that heat, sweating and hungry, I was kicking myself for taking the letter back. How was I going to go to Manzanar? It wasn't till I got to the station that I realized I didn't even have enough money for a ticket to Bakersfield.

The station and the platform were crowded with soldiers standing around and sitting on the floor and against the walls. I walked up and down outside, talking to myself. What was I going to do now? I should have taken the money when Mr. Mori offered it.

A tall colored sailor sitting on a duffel bag was watching me. "Hey, sailor," he said. I touched the cap and nodded. "Too hot to be out there in the sun," he said. "Sit down and take a load off."

I squatted down next to him. "I have to get to Bakersfield, but I'm flat broke. You think I can get on the train anyway?"

"I wouldn't count on it," he said. "What's your name?"
"Adam Pelko."

"I'm Jerry Thomas." He got to his feet and tucked in his navy blouse. "I'm going inside there, Adam, to see what's going on with that train. I've been waiting here for six hours. Keep an eye on my duffel."

"I don't mind."

When he came back, he handed me half a chocolate bar. "The train is still stuck up the line somewhere. It's all those troop trains coming through. I've got to get to L.A. tonight. My leave's up at midnight."

"What are you going to do?" I licked chocolate off my fingers.

He pointed to a freight train standing on the other side of the tracks. "I've been watching that train. It came in here a while ago. Soon as they couple up an engine, that's my ride."

"Is it going to Bakersfield?"

"It's sure pointed that way."

"Can I go with you?"

"Hey, little brother, be my guest."

Later we crossed the tracks and made our way around the end of the freight train. "Act normal," Jerry said. "We're just minding our own business. You never know how a crew's going to be. Once the train starts moving, we move. Just follow me. Do what I do, and you'll be fine."

The engine whistled twice, the cars stirred, and then, one after another, like a row of dominoes, they jarred forward. We walked along with the slowly moving train. As it began picking up speed Jerry started running, the duffel bouncing on his shoulder.

He heaved the bag into an open boxcar and swung himself up, then reached out to me. I grabbed his hand and ran along with the train. "Jump, man!" he said.

I got myself halfway in and Jerry pulled me in the rest of the way. I lay there catching my breath. "That was something," I said. "I never did that before."

"Good man," he said.

21

The boxcar must have been full of potatoes. A few were still rolling around. I picked one up and gnawed on it. "You that hungry?" Jerry said. "Me, I like my potatoes home fried and scrambled with eggs."

"Me too," I said, and tossed the potato aside.

We sat in the open door looking out at the passing trees and the fields that kept changing colors. I leaned back on my elbows. The sun was going down, big as a peach on the horizon. The whistle blew at every crossing. A boy stuck his head out a car window and waved to us.

"Feels good to move, doesn't it?" Jerry said. He dug a pint bottle out of his duffel bag, unscrewed the top, and took a swallow. "That's the ticket."

He offered me the bottle. I'd had sips of different drinks with my parents, but never straight whiskey. It went down a little warm, but nice, a taste like vanilla.

The sun sank, the light flattening out, softening. We went past two boys spearing frogs. "Helloooo," I called out.

"You ever hear of Crispus Attucks?" Jerry asked.

"Who's that?"

"A colored man who died for the American Revolution. That was the Boston Massacre he died at. There's a statue of him in Boston."

"I never heard of him."

"They don't teach you history straight. Do you know the biggest hero of Pearl Harbor was a Negro? Doris Miller. Mess boy like me, but he got a gun and brought those Japs down single handed."

"I saw him," I said. "He was on the *West Virginia*, right?"

"You saw Doris Miller? Come on! What was a kid like you doing on a battleship? I think that bourbon got to you."

"It's the truth. I was on the *Westy*, and I saw this colored sailor shooting a machine gun."

"You telling me you really saw the man?"

"Sure did." The drink had made me a little woozy, and I lay back, listening to the *clickety-clickety-clack* of the wheels on the rails.

"How about that?" Jerry said. "I'm sitting next to someone who saw Doris Miller. You're a piece of history, man." He was sitting up, smoking. "Wish I was going home, but somebody hits you, you gotta hit 'em back. Somebody kills you, you gotta kill them back."

I dozed off while Jerry was still talking. The next thing I knew, he shook me awake. "Come on, Adam, we've got to Lindy."

The train had slowed down. He pushed his duffel out the door and jumped after it. I looked out into the darkness, then jumped, my feet bicycling as I hit the ground. A moment later Jerry found me. "That was good, little brother."

The freight train had pulled off on a siding. We hid in the bushes and watched the trainman go past, swinging his lantern and checking the cars.

A troop train hurtled by on the main line. I caught glimpses of soldiers through the windows, jackets off, ties undone, heard their voices, scraps of music, everything rushing by, disappearing into the darkness. After the last car passed, we climbed back into the boxcar.

A half hour later the train stopped again to let another military train pass. We didn't bother getting off.

The third time the train stopped, we got caught. A trainman pinned us in the light from his lantern. "How many of you in here?"

"Just us two sailor boys," Jerry said.

"What are your names?"

"I'm Jerry Thomas, and this here is Adam . . ."

"Pelko," I said.

The trainman swung his lantern, looking up and down the track, then he looked in the car again. "Just the two of you? You look pretty young to be in the service, Adam."

"Yes, sir." I thought he was going to throw me off.

"I've got a ship to catch in L.A. tonight," Jerry said. "You think I can make it?"

"You're never going to get there on this clunker." The trainman pulled a watch on a chain from a pocket of his overalls. "Okay, this is what you've got to do, sailors. We'll be in the Bakersfield yards in twenty minutes. You guys hightail it to the station and catch the L.A. train."

"Well, thank you, sir," Jerry said. "We appreciate that."

"I know what it is. I've got a boy in the service too. About like Adam here."

"Sir," I said, "how would I get to Manzanar?"

"I thought you were going to L.A."

"No, sir. Manzanar. Not right away, but I will be."

"Manzanar, that's up there in the Owens Valley." He signaled with his lantern, raising and lowering it several times. "Anytime you're ready to go, you come find me in the Bakersfield yards. Just ask for Mike Jiminez. Ask anybody. I'll take care of you."

22

In the Bakersfield freight yards Jerry had to run for his train. I just had time to say good-bye. "Hey, Jerry," I yelled after him. "Bye! Thanks!" He turned and waved, and I watched him till he was out of sight. I wondered if I'd ever see him again.

I made my way across the tracks. The sky was dark with low-hanging clouds. It was late, and I ran all the way home.

The house was lit up, and people were sitting around on the steps and the porch railing, drinking and talking. It looked as if everyone was out there, waiting for me. Some-one had set up a Victrola, and there was music. Both Mrs. LaValley and Mom were dancing with men I didn't recog-nize. I thought I could slip up to my room, but the minute Mom saw me, she broke away from her partner, came down the steps, and grabbed my arm.

"You were gone all day." She shook my arm. "How dare you go off like that without a word to me."

"Mom . . . Mom." I tried to put my arm around her. "Nothing happened. I'm here, I'm home. No broken bones, see?"

"Don't be joking with me, Adam. You can't walk in with not even a do-re-mi and act like it's nothing."

"I'm sorry. I was doing things. The time got away from me and—"

"Please! Don't say another thing. I can't stand it when you lie to me. I know where you were. Nancy told me."

"She told you what?"

"What you should have told me yourself, that you went to Fresno with that Woody character. And after I told you not to. I can't believe you would do that and not say anything to me."

"Because you'd never agree."

"You're right, but that doesn't allow you to go off anytime you want and do anything you please."

"I'm not a baby, Mom. I'm not Bea. I don't have to report in every five minutes."

"I can't talk to you now. I'm too angry and upset. Please go upstairs."

"So you can go back to your boyfriend," I muttered.

"What did you say? What gives you the right to talk to me like that? Go on, go!"

I had to walk past everyone, all of them acting like they hadn't been listening. Mrs. LaValley, who was still dancing, gave me a little smile.

Upstairs in my room I could still hear them laughing and talking. I hated them all, but especially my mother for humiliating me in front of everyone. If she was so upset, why was she out there dancing? When was the last time she'd even talked about my father? It was all just her job and her new friends and "Keep an eye on Bea" and "Tell me everything you're thinking and doing." Did she even think about Dad anymore? Did I?

Yes! Yes, I did. But not like before. Sometimes hours could pass and I didn't think about him at all. The thought made me hate myself.

The next morning when I got back from the dairy, I went over to see Nancy. She was outside, standing on a kitchen chair, rigging a clothesline from a tree to a corner of their house. "Hi," she said. "How'd it go in Fresno?"

"A total bust. For starters, Woody's car burned up. He took all my money, and then he dumped me out on the highway. And now my mother's so mad at me she won't even talk to me. Why did you have to tell her where I went?"

"Adam, she came over here and asked me if you went to Fresno. She said it like that. 'Did he go to Fresno?'"

"You could have said you didn't know."

"Sorry, I wasn't going to lie to her for you."

"Yeah, I'm the only one who tells lies. You really fixed me good."

"Hey!" She jumped off the chair. "Don't put it on me. You're the one who went there."

"You encouraged me. You said I should do it."

She shrugged. "I didn't make you do it, Adam. You want to be mad, be mad at Woody. Or be mad at yourself. And why don't you just take your ugly mug away from here now and come back when you're in a better mood."

"Fine!" I said, and I walked off.

I had the rest of the day to stew. I kept thinking about what I was going to say to my mother. *Why do you always have to be right, and I'm always wrong?*

My father always had to be right too, but he was the father. When he and Mom disagreed, he made the decision. Now she thought she could step into his shoes, but she was wrong. Nobody could do that.

I was going to tell her that, too, but I never had a chance. A minute after I heard her ride dropping her off after work, she was on the way up to my room in the attic, clumping up the stairs in her work boots. She started right in on me.

"Maybe you think something's changed in this family, Adam, and now you're in charge and you can do anything you want. I have news for you, Adam. From now on I don't want to hear anything from you, especially your opinions about what I should or shouldn't be doing."

"Mom . . . Mom—"

"Not a word!" She turned around and went back down the stairs.

I felt like jumping out of the window. What did I come home for? I should have just kept going to Manzanar when I had the chance.

At supper Bea kept asking, "What did Adam do? Was he bad?"

"Eat your food," I said, "and mind your own business." I

was mad at everyone—Nancy for blabbing, Woody for being an idiot, even Davi for sticking that letter on me.

Bea was the only one I couldn't stay mad at. She followed me up to my room after supper. "You were mean to me," she said.

"I know. That wasn't fair. It's Mom I'm mad at. You're the only one who likes me, anyway."

"Mommy likes you," Bea said. "She's just tired from all her jobs. She has too much responsibility."

"Responsibility, huh? Do you even know what the word means?"

"It means you have to go to work early in the morning."

"You know everything, don't you?"

"Not everything. I have a lot of things to learn still."

"Like what?"

"Spelling words, reading, um . . . um . . . but I can tie my own shoes. What's that?" She pointed to Davi's letter where I'd left it on top of the radio. "This letter," she said, picking it up, "is from that friend Davi. Is it the one about his father?"

"Yes, that letter." I put it back on the radio, thinking that if Mom knew I was going to Manzanar to bring this to Davi's father, she'd never talk to me again.

23

I went back to the railroad yards outside of Bakersfield, looking for that trainman, Mike Jiminez, so he could tell me how to get to Manzanar. I was just coming across the tracks when I saw Babe Gribble on a path next to the parking lot, throwing stones at a post. I hadn't seen him since school ended, and I wasn't glad to see him now.

I was going to go the other way, but he looked around and saw me, and he waved. Waved? Babe Gribble? I shrugged and waved back.

"Pesko," he yelled. "Come over here."

"Pelko." Was he going to start that again? "What do you want?"

"What are you doing here, Pelko?"

"What do I need, permission from you?"

"You're not supposed to be walking on the tracks."

"Says who?"

"Says me."

"You in charge of this place too?"

"My father's the stationmaster. And he don't want kids

walking all over the tracks and getting killed. I could have you kicked off in a second."

"Okay, Mr. Big Shot."

"Me? You're the big shot. The big war expert. You think you know everything. You think you're the only one who knows about war because your father got it at Pearl Harbor."

"I never said anything like that."

"You don't know nothing. How many you got serving from your family? You know how many I got?" He held up five fingers. "Five," he said, in case I couldn't count. "Five, plus two uncles. I've got one in the Philippines with General MacArthur. And one in England. And my brother's in North Africa."

"That's good," I said, picking up a handful of gravel and letting it fly.

"Good is right. My family is just as important as yours."

"I never said they weren't."

He stood there glaring at me. "My brother's missing in action."

"Huh," I said. "That's tough for your family."

"I didn't say he was dead, Pelko, just missing. If those Germans grabbed him, they better look out. Missing? What does that mean? My brother's tough. He's out there some-where. Maybe he joined up with the French foreign legion. They're right there, in Africa."

"Sure," I said, remembering how I had wanted to believe

my father was only missing, not dead. "You never know. Your brother's probably all right. They pulled guys out of the water for weeks after Pearl Harbor. I mean, they said they were missing, and then they found them."

"That's right, Pelko, and they're going to find my brother."

"That's right," I said.

"You come around here a lot?"

"Sometimes. I'm looking for somebody. How about you?"

"I'm waiting for my father to get off work. Who you looking for? I know everybody around here. What's his name?"

"Mike Jiminez."

"Oh, him. Stay there. I'll ask in the office, see if he's here."

I leaned against a post and waited. I liked the yards, the smell of the coal and the big, black, huffing steam engines, and the trains carrying nothing but military equipment. When you were here, you knew there was a war on.

Babe didn't come right back, and I began to think he'd played another one of his nasty tricks on me. I never expected him to do anything for me anyway.

"Found him!" Babe threw up his arm. "I told you I'd get him, Pesko."

"Pelko," I muttered.

"Okay," he said. "Mike Jiminez is on his regular run. He's here every other day. He's coming in around seven tonight. He'll be in the yard office. How do you know him, anyway?"

"I'll tell you the next time I see you. Seven o'clock? I've got to go." I ran for home. I didn't have much time. If Mike Jiminez could put me on a train tonight, I was going to do it and get it over with and worry about Mom later.

She was making supper and listening to the news on the radio when I got home. "Hi," I said.

She looked up and nodded. "Supper's ready."

"Where's Bea?"

"She's playing with the little Blaine girl. I fed her early. Sit down." Mom served me, then sat down with her food. After a moment she said, "What did you do today?"

"Nothing much. I worked this morning. Talked to Nancy." I left out the yards and Mike Jiminez and Manzanar. Not really lying, but not telling the truth, either.

In my room I wrote a note and left it on my pillow.

> *Mom,*
> *I have to deliver Davi's letter. Going to Manzanar.*
> *Sorry. I'll be home as soon as I can. Don't worry.*

I picked up my cap and Davi's letter and went downstairs. "Going out," I called, and I was out the door before she could say anything.

I found Mike Jiminez in the yard office, just as Babe had said. He was sitting at a wooden table with some papers.

"Wait a minute, Adam," he said, like he'd seen me yesterday. "I just want to finish this report."

I perched on the bench, and I thought about calling Mom. At least she wouldn't be able to say I'd gone off without a word, but then Mike Jiminez was on his feet. "Let's go," he said, taking his lantern.

It was getting dark, and the circle of light from his lantern swung forward and back. We crossed several tracks to where a massive black engine was being backed up to a long line of freight cars.

"This is the young fellow I told you about," Mike Jiminez said to the brakeman.

"Okay." The brakeman beckoned us to follow him along the line of cars. He flashed his light into an empty car. "Climb in," he said. It was that easy.

"You're all set now, Adam," Mike Jiminez said. "Just stay put. You'll know you're there when you see the snow on Mount Whitney." He slid the door half shut, then the two men stood outside talking.

I felt around in the dark until I found some empty burlap bags, and sat down. I could still get off, go home. Mom wouldn't know I'd even thought about going to Manzanar. The train started with a jerk, and my head hit the wall. It was done. I was on my way.

I must have fallen asleep. When I woke up, the door was shut tight and it was pitch dark. I could feel the engine straining and the wheels grinding against the rails. I slept on and off through the night. Toward morning the cold woke me. A cutting wind was coming through every crack in the boxcar. I wrapped a burlap bag around my shoulders and threw another across my legs.

When it started to get light, I got up and pulled the door open. Cold air rushed in. Soot peppered my arms. We were moving across a wide, empty plain, sliding almost effortlessly along the edge of the mountains. I don't know what it was—maybe the way we were skating across the plain—but I felt like I had entered another world, and in that dim early light I saw the mountains turn into a line of battleships and my father standing on the bridge. It was only a moment. The light changed and he disappeared.

The train rolled on, past black rocks and white salt flats and big cottonwood trees and long, skinny poplars. As the sun came up, the mountains kept changing color, gray in one light, then pink, then glittering gold.

The train slowed, then stopped. I jumped off, then climbed the narrow metal ladder between the cars for a better look. Ahead I saw the engine and the tender behind it, under a water tower, and Mount Whitney, higher than all the others, covered with snow. The track seemed to be running straight toward it.

All the rest of the way across the valley I leaned out the door, watching for the Manzanar station. When the train slowed again, I saw a station and jumped off and waited for the train to pass. The sun was up now, and I was hot and thirsty.

The sign on the station read LONE PINE, not MANZANAR.

The building was locked, and there was no one around. A faded poster in the window said FOR VICTORY, BUY UNITED STATES WAR BONDS. I tried the door even though I could see that the place was empty.

I sat down on the platform, hoping somebody would show up. Why hadn't I brought sandwiches with me? Why was I here? Why hadn't I listened to Mom? Why had I jumped off the train? I was so hungry I started chewing on my nails. I didn't have even a crumb in my pockets. A row of big, juicy black ants marched alongside my foot. I grabbed one, ready to take a bite out of it, but it nipped me first and I let go of it fast.

I found a water spigot around the side of the building. At first the water ran rusty and hot, but it cooled, and I plunged my hands and head into it, washing and drinking at the same time. Then I went back to the platform and waited.

I stared at Mount Whitney. It didn't exactly stare back at me, but it sat there, bigger than everything. Looking at that mountain, I felt like one of those black ants.

As the sun rose higher it got really hot. I went back to the water spigot and drenched myself again, then sat in the shade. It was midmorning when I saw a car coming toward the station, kicking up a trail of dust. I jumped to my feet, yelling and waving.

An old man got out of the car—it was a Model A Ford— and started lifting a box from the open rumble seat. "Let me do that for you, sir." I ran over and lifted it out for him. It wasn't half as heavy as a milk can.

"Put it on the platform, son," he said. "Near the door."

"You waiting for the train?" the old woman with him said.

"I want to go to Manzanar, ma'am. Is it far?"

"Not that far," the man said. "Somebody coming for you?"

"No, sir, but I can walk. Just tell me which way to go."

"We'll run you over there," the woman said. She pointed to the rumble seat, and I climbed in. Then she handed me a bag of sunflower seeds. "Eat up," she said. "Boys are always hungry. You got somebody over there?"

"It's my friend's father."

She nodded. "Oh, one of the guards. Chester," she yelled to the old man. "He's got a friend who's a guard over there."

"Uh-huh."

The road was rough, and wind and dust blew in my face, but it was exciting riding out in the open, watching the mountains and spitting sunflower seeds. For a while the old man drove parallel to the mountains, then at a turnoff he pulled over. A sign swinging in the wind said MANZANAR WAR RELOCATION CENTER.

"We go back the other way," the man said. "You can walk from here."

"I'm sorry I ate all your sunflower seeds," I said to the woman.

"Now, now. That's what they're for," she said, and she handed me an apple.

"Thank you," I said. "Thank you for the ride."

"Just follow the road," the man said. "It's not far."

I started walking toward Manzanar, eating the apple. The wind sprang up and a cloud of yellow dust rolled toward me. In a moment the weather changed. The sun disappeared. Twigs and brush whipped against my legs, grit filled my mouth, and I could barely see the road. I sat down with my back to the wind, pulled down my cap to protect my face, and curled my arms over my head.

24

I was hunched over, collar up, my father's cap pulled down over my face, when I saw something coming at me, something shadowy, no shape, like a bodiless ghost blowing this way and that. It hovered over me. "Hello, haole," it said.

I wiped the dust out of my eyes and sat up. "Davi?"

It was Davi.

Davi, a rag tied over his mouth, hair flying, wearing a khaki army shirt so big it was blowing around him like a sail. It was Davi, bigger than I remembered, but Davi, all right.

"Adam," he said. "What are you doing here?"

And that's the way we met, in the middle of nowhere, in the middle of a dust storm, the whole sky dark, on a road that kept disappearing.

We went wild, dancing around. "How'd you get here?" he said.

"Where'd you come from?" I said.

"You were sitting there like a bump on a log," Davi said. "I walked right up to you, and you didn't say a word. You didn't even recognize me."

"I knew it was you. You said, 'Hello, haole.' Nobody else calls me haole."

"I didn't say 'haole.' I said, 'aloha.' Hello! Hello, that's what I said. Hello, you haole jerk. And how did you know I was here?"

"I didn't know. What's that?" I pointed to the snake he had draped around his neck. It must have been four feet long. "Is it alive?"

Davi held it up. "Isn't that a beauty? It's a diamondback rattler."

"A rattlesnake? You found it?"

"And killed it. It's for my father. It's going to be a soup, to give him strength."

"Davi. Why didn't you write and say you were here? You know why I'm here?" I pulled the letter out of my pocket. "I'm here to give your father this letter."

"Oh, that."

"Yes, *that*," I said.

"I was going to write you, Adam. We haven't been here that long. We're all here now with my dad, my whole family. My parents, my sister, and her kids and her husband." He punched me on the arm. "And now you're here too."

"With the letter," I said, meaning to slap it into his hand, but the wind took it, and it blew away.

25

"Where have you been, young Mori?" a man with his head wrapped in a rag called from the back of a green army truck loaded with wood and branches.

"Look what I got." Davi held up the snake. "And look what else I got. My friend Adam."

"Is that snake alive? I wouldn't put it past you. Come on, get in. We want to get out of here."

A soldier put his head out the cab window. "Who you got there, Mori?"

"My cousin," Davi said. "He got lost."

The soldier barely glanced at me. "Get in back, both of you. Let's go."

The men made a place for us, and in a few minutes we were at the Manzanar gate, and a guard waved the truck through.

I helped Davi and the men unload the truck. They worked steadily, but I kept looking around. Manzanar had been just a word to me, a strange word, but now I saw it, bigger than I had imagined. It was like an army camp, full of people and buildings.

"Let's go," Davi said. "I want my folks to see you. They won't believe their eyes."

We cleaned up at a nearby washroom. I kept rinsing my mouth and spitting out dirt. "Is it always like this?" I said as we went outside.

"What's the matter, you don't like dirt?" Davi said. "Come on, this way."

We walked down a wide firebreak, past block after block of tar-papered barracks. Finally Davi pointed to one of the barracks. "That's us."

We went into a room divided with sheets and blankets thrown over clotheslines strung from wall to wall. I caught a glimpse of people behind a sheet. "Who're they?" I whispered.

"Not my family," Davi said. "They just live here." He lifted another sheet. "Here we are. Hey, Sam," he said to a man lying on a cot in his underwear, a cloth over his face. "Here's my friend Adam."

Sam raised a corner of the cloth. "Hello." He pointed to the snake Davi had over his shoulder. "What've you got there?"

"Dinner for Pop."

"You're going nuts again. You know this nut?" he said to me. "You must be as crazy as we are to come to this place," and he let the cloth drop over his face.

"That's my brother-in-law," Davi said. "And that's my sister." She was sitting on the bed fanning a little girl in her lap. "Janet, this is Adam Pelko. Remember I told you about him?"

"Hello," I said. It was embarrassing. It was like being in someone's bedroom.

"Hello, Adam. I know all about you," Janet said.

"Nothing but the truth," Davi said. "That little devil on her lap, Adam, is Esther Williams Harada. And the goofball playing with the truck is Georgie." Davi's nephew had a handkerchief tied over his face too. "Who are you today," Davi said, "Jesse James?"

All this time I'd been hearing the wind. Each time it gusted, the windows rattled and sand blew in.

Davi lifted another sheet, and we squeezed into his parents' part of the room. His father was sitting on a stool, the smoke from a cigarette curling around his face. He didn't look at me or say anything. Mrs. Mori, who was mending a dress, smoothed a place on the bed and gestured for me to sit down.

"It's okay, Mama," Davi said, "we're just here for a minute. Pop, look who's here. It's Adam. He came to see you. Remember you fixed his bike?"

"Hello, Mr. Mori," I said. I almost didn't recognize him. He looked sick. I remembered the way he had jumped off the back of his truck, like a boy.

"Look what I brought you, Pop." Davi spread the snake across his father's lap. His father put down his cigarette, and they examined the snake together, Davi with his hand on his father's shoulder. "It'll make a good stew, Pop, right?" Davi said, and his father answered in Japanese.

I stood there watching them, and my head started

burning. I told myself it was the heat and being in this place, this strange place where I didn't belong.

I kept watching Davi and his father. There they were together. In this ugly, dusty place, but together. Together, the way I would never be with my father.

I couldn't stay.

I didn't say anything. I just left, pushing the sheets aside and rushing out.

I ran. Ran past rows of barracks, ran till I was up against the wire fence and had to stop.

I sat down on a boulder near some spindly trees, and all I wanted was to be out of this place. Gone. Away. I didn't want to see Davi. I didn't want to see his father. I didn't want to see them together.

I'd done what I said I would do. *Right, Dad?* I'd been looking for Davi's father, and he was here. Maybe I hadn't exactly found him, but he was here and Davi was here, and they had each other.

And me? What did I have? All this morning, ever since I'd awakened on the train and seen this new country, this place I'd never been, I'd been excited, looking up at the mountains as if my father were there. There was something in me that wouldn't give up, couldn't stop hoping.

26

"What did you run out for?" Davi asked. I'd hopped off the rock the minute I saw him, and now we were walking along the fence. "You mad at me or something?"

"No."

"You sure?"

I looked at him. I knew I should say something. This was Davi, my best friend, but I had nothing to say. There was nothing to say. What was, was.

"I have to go home, Davi. I missed work this morning. I've probably lost my job."

"You just got here, Adam."

"I'll come back another time."

"No, you won't," he said. "Why would anyone come here if they didn't have to? Stay. I'll find you a ride tomorrow."

Tomorrow? I'd already been gone one night away from home. Now two nights? I could hardly imagine what my mother would think. She'd be ready to kill me. Or kick me out of the house. What a mess. The whole thing was so stupid. I'd come all this way to deliver a letter that nobody cared about anymore. I was glad to see Davi. I guess I was glad. I wasn't sure about that or anything else right now. And how was I going to get home, anyway?

"Who's going to give me a ride?" I asked Davi.

"Don't worry, there are trucks going in and out of here all day."

I finally just had to shut up about it. "What do we do now?" I asked.

"What do you want to do?"

"Eat."

"They don't open the mess hall for another hour. Just hope they don't have liver tonight."

"I haven't eaten all day, Davi. Can't I get some food here?"

"Take it easy, Adam. You're going to get fed. What do you think, we live on sand?"

We walked around talking. Davi was showing me stuff and telling me things about the school and the gardens people were making, and I was going, "Uh-huh, uh-huh." Davi should have left me alone. It wasn't his fault. It was me thinking about him and his father, the same thing over and over again, him and his father, and me with nothing. It was stupid. Even as I thought it I knew it was stupid. Davi and his father were prisoners here, and I was free.

"Here's the rec hall," he said, stopping in front of another tar-papered building. "You want to play Ping-Pong?"

"Maybe later."

"You don't have much to say," Davi said. "I never knew you were such a silent guy."

"I'll feel better when I get some food in me," I said.

"Soon," Davi said. "Let's go get in line."

At the mess hall a stocky guy jeered at Davi, "Chowhound!"

"Hamanaka," Davi said. "You're standing in front of us."

"Who's the round-eyes?" Hamanaka pointed to me.

"My cousin from Honolulu."

"Very funny. Mori's got a sense of humor."

They went back and forth that way. Davi was still the way he was in Honolulu, a mouthy guy, but different, too, like nothing could get to him.

And I was different too, but a different kind of different. Different from everybody here. "I don't belong here," I said to Davi.

"Nobody belongs here. Don't worry, you're not the only haole in here. Round-eyes marry slanty-eyes, and even though round-eyes don't have to come here, they come because they want to stay with their families. Get it?"

"Got it."

That night we slept in the bachelors' barracks, a big, unfinished open space. "Why don't you stay with your family?" I asked.

"Where would I sleep, under the floor?"

We pulled our cots away from the others so we could talk after the lights went out. "So, what do you think of our country club now?" Davi said. "Those mountains—"

"That's a million-dollar view," I said. For a moment it was like it used to be, the two of us making fun of everything.

"And how about that fence and those towers and those searchlights? Keeps the riffraff out. We're an exclusive club, so don't bother applying, Adam."

We were both quiet for a while. It had cooled a lot and I was glad for the blanket. The barrack was dark now, except for a single lightbulb burning at the other end. I kicked Davi's cot. "You sleeping?"

"No."

"What are you thinking about, your father?"

"I always think about him."

"Me too. I think about my father all the time."

"I'm thinking what they did to him," Davi said, "the way they treated him like a traitor. For nothing. They put him in prison for nothing. He never says anything, but it hurts him."

"It's a rotten deal."

"Yes, it is," he said. "And sometimes he feels so bad nobody can help him, except my mom. He starts yelling, and she's the only one who can get him quiet. She got him doing things, digging up a garden, making furniture. You know how he is, he can do anything with his hands."

I leaned up on one elbow. "Your mother didn't recognize me."

"She knew you. She was just too polite to say anything. That's the way the older ones are. She doesn't want anything that will draw attention to us. She says the nail that sticks up gets the hammer. She says we just have to be patient, one day it will end and we'll go home. That's okay for them, but not me. I'm American. I shouldn't be here."

"I know it," I said.

"I'll tell you something. The farmers around here are desperate for pickers. All their regular workers are in the army. A lot of people from here have gone out to work on the farms. I've gone out, and I'm going to go out again, and one of these times, Adam"—he came over to my cot and lowered his voice—"I'm gonna go, and I'm not coming back."

"Davi, that's crazy." I grabbed his arm. "There're guys out there who'll shoot you, as soon as look at you. I'm not kidding. I told you what happened to me outside of Fresno. That guy said 'Jap,' and if it had been you, he would have killed you."

"Jap," Davi repeated.

"I didn't say it. It was that drunk. Here's my idea," I said, sitting up. "We stay in school until we're seventeen, and then if the war's still on, we join up."

"I don't know," he said. "A lot of guys here say they'll never join up as long as they keep us in this place. Why should we fight when they treat us like traitors? But some guys say we should join if they let us, it's our country. We gotta show we're as patriotic as anyone."

"Well, what do you think?"

"I don't know. I'm thinking about it. Ask me next year."

"I don't see that there's anything to think about," I said. "We're at war. You can be mad about the government, but when your country's attacked, when it needs you, you have to serve. You don't say 'Maybe I will and maybe I won't.'"

"My country? I know it's my country," Davi said. "I don't need you to tell me that. But what about this place? What about what they did to my father?"

"What about what they did to my father?"

"Who are you talking about?" he said, jumping up.

"The Japs!" I said, and I was on my feet too. "The Japs killed him!"

"The *Japs*?" he repeated, pushing me.

"You know what I mean." I grabbed his arm and held him. "You saw them! You were with me. You saw the planes. You saw the bombs. You saw my father's ship go down!"

"You think it was me on one of those planes?" He shoved me away and got back in bed.

"I'm not saying that. I'm not blaming you," I said.

He didn't answer. He didn't speak to me again, and I couldn't fall asleep for a long time. I lay there going over and over the whole stupid day. My father . . . his father . . . what I'd said . . . what Davi had said. . . .

I shouldn't have said "Jap," but he knew I didn't mean him. It was the country where his parents were born. If his parents hadn't come to Hawaii, Davi would have been born there too. I lay there looking up into the dark, thinking, *Yes, it could have been him on one of those planes.*

27

In the morning when I got up, Davi was gone. I got dressed and went outside. The mountains gleamed at me, sharp as teeth. I went looking for Davi and got lost. This place spread in every direction, and everywhere it was the same—barracks and more barracks, and people and more people. They couldn't all be enemies. Now, in the morning light, the way I'd felt last night was crazy. I was just afraid that Davi was still mad.

"Adam!" Davi caught up to me and put his arm around my shoulders.

"I was looking for you," I said.

"I saw you. Didn't you hear me calling you? Come on, we're eating with my parents. We're not going to the mess hall this morning."

His mother had set a folding table outside their barrack, and his family was all together. Davi kissed his mother and sat down on the bench next to his father.

"Caucasian boy," his father said, and pointed with his cigarette to the place opposite him. I sat down, and Mrs. Mori passed me a bowl with rice and something I didn't recognize.

"He's not going to eat Japanese food for breakfast, Mom," Davi said. "Don't you have any cornflakes?"

"I don't mind," I said. "It looks good."

"Rattlesnake stew," Davi said, and started laughing.

I ate it just to show him.

I was almost finished eating when Davi's father said, "Caucasian boy, for you." He handed me a small, polished black stone.

"He finds stones in the fields," Davi said, "and he polishes them. He says they're a piece of the mountain."

I turned the stone over and over. It was warm, and it felt just right in my hand, like it belonged there.

"For you," Mr. Mori said. "*Genki-de.*"

I looked at Davi.

"He's thanking you," Davi said.

"What for?"

"For coming here, for caring about my family."

Mr. Mori nodded. "The journey. Here, to this place."

I stood up. I closed my hand over the stone. "I'll keep it forever." I wanted to say something else. It was as if Davi's father knew what I had been feeling and had given me not only a stone, not only a piece of the mountain, but himself, as if he was sharing himself with me, doing for me what a father does. "*Genki-de,*" I said. "*Genki-de,* Mr. Mori."

28

Davi and I went to the office near the main gate so I could get a pass to leave. "Who's this?" the man in the office asked.

"Adam Pelko," I said, and I started to explain, but Davi interrupted with a story about being on the wood detail yesterday and finding me wandering around in the dust storm. "He was lost, so we brought him in."

"You should have come directly to the office," the man grumbled, but he wrote out the pass.

"I knew he would," Davi said. when we were outside. "What else could he do? They weren't going to keep you here."

"You just made that up, that whole story."

"I wasn't going to say you came to see me. They'd think you were a spy or something."

Trucks were lined up on the road. "I think I can get you on that mail truck," Davi said.

We went over to talk to the driver. He had a snake tattoo wound around one arm and a hula girl on the other. "I'm willing," he said, "but I got a bunch of stops to make along the way. It's going to take a while to get to Bakersfield, but I'll get you there. Just give me a few minutes to pick up the mail, and I'll be ready to go."

"I wish you were coming with me," I said to Davi. I fingered the stone in my pocket. "Remember what we talked about. I don't want you to do anything stupid."

"I don't do stupid things."

"I know. I mean, like disappearing."

He wriggled his fingers at me, like they were flyaway wings. Like, *Bye-bye, baby*. Like if he wanted to go, he'd go no matter what I said.

The truck driver beeped the horn, and I climbed into the cab and rolled down the window. Then, without thinking about it, I tossed my father's Zippo lighter to Davi.

"What's this for?" he said.

"It's for you. I've got your father's stone. Now you've got my father's lighter. Are you going to write?"

"Are you?"

"I will, if you will."

"If you will, I will."

We were stopped at the gate, and then we drove through. "Davi!" I called. I kept looking back. The last I saw, Davi was still standing there, looking out from the other side of the fence.

29

It was dark when I got home. My mother was in the kitchen. "Hi, Mom," I said, and gave her a smile. "Anything to eat?"

She looked at me for a moment. "There's the refrigerator." She struck a match on the stove and lit a cigarette.

I looked in the refrigerator. "What should I take?"

"Take what you want."

I took out the meatloaf. "Can I eat this?"

"Why not?" She got an ashtray and sat down and watched as I cut a slice of meatloaf and got the bread.

"Do you want some of this?" I asked.

"We ate."

I sat down, then I had to get up and get a plate. Then the ketchup. Then a knife and fork. And all the time Mom watched, not saying a word. I put the fork down. "What?" I said.

"You tell me."

"Didn't you see my note? Mom, I'm sorry."

"You're not sorry. Or maybe you are, but it doesn't mean anything. You did what you wanted to do. Anyway, what are you sorry about?"

"For worrying you."

"Don't worry about me. You better worry about yourself." She stubbed out the cigarette.

"I know you didn't want me to go, but—"

"Adam. Listen to yourself. You did just what you wanted to do, and now you want me to make it all nice."

"Do you want to know what happened, why I had to stay an extra night?"

"No."

"Mom, what do you want me to say?"

"Say anything you want."

"Well . . . I thought you'd be proud of me."

"Proud of you? What for? For worrying me to death? For keeping me up two nights? For not knowing where you were or what was happening to you?"

"No, not that. I'm sorry about that!"

"Don't give me that 'I'm sorry' stuff. Just remember, Adam, actions speak louder than words. Actions have consequences."

"What consequences, Mom? Nothing's happened. Mission accomplished. It's all over."

"It sure is." She stood up and left the room.

I started up to my room, then I went back down again and put the food away and the dishes in the sink. I looked around. *Done? Not yet. Better wash those dishes. And dry them. And put them away.*

All the time I was cleaning up, I was talking to her in my head. *I knew you'd be mad at me, but you'd be proud, too. I really*

carried out my mission. Okay, it wasn't your mission, not any-
thing you wanted me to do, but I set out to do something, and I did
it. I thought that counted for something in this family.

Up in my room I moped around, looking out the window
thinking about Mom and Davi, and Davi and Mom, and
Davi . . . and then I had a really great idea.

A great idea!

I sat right down and wrote Davi a letter.

August 5, 1942

Dear Davi,

*I have a great idea for you. My grandfather has a
dairy farm near Watertown, New York, and he always
needs help. Remember I told you about the snow there,
how it piles up ten feet every winter? Here's my idea—
you can live with him, go to school there, and help around
the farm, but the main thing is,* you'd be out of Manzanar. *I'm writing my grandfather right now. I know
he's going to say yes. What do you say?*

Your friend,

Adam

30

"You're fired," Mr. Medina said the next morning when I came in to work. He was loading the empty milk cans onto the back of the truck.

"I'll do that, Mr. Medina." I picked up a can and handed it up to him.

"You're late. Two days late, and I'm doing your job." He jammed the cans together. "I don't need that kind of help. I need somebody reliable."

I kept handing milk cans up to him. "What are you doing?" he said.

"I'm working."

"I'm not paying you."

"That's okay. I swear, it's not going to happen again."

"Don't bother swearing. Nobody's listening. Get in the truck. We're late enough already."

In the truck I was quiet as a mouse. I didn't speak until he did.

"Where were you," he asked, "fooling around with your girlfriend?"

"I don't have a girlfriend."

"Don't tell me that. I have eyes. I see that girl who comes around here."

"She's just a friend, Mr. Medina." I didn't want him to think I wasn't serious.

"So, what's your excuse for missing two days of work?"

"I have this friend who comes from Hawaii. His name is Davi Mori—"

"What are you talking about now?" he said.

"It's about the Japanese," I said. "Do you know what happened to the Japanese here, how the government moved them all?"

"Sure, I know. You think I'm ignorant? My daughter-in-law is Japanese. She and my son are worried stiff."

"Are they in Manzanar?"

"No, and they're not going there either. And stop talking about it. Forget I said anything. They don't need some dumb kid shooting his mouth off about them." He pulled the truck alongside the first farm platform. "Get those cans."

I jumped out, pulled the empties off the truck, and loaded the full cans. I hustled like that all morning. When we got back to the dairy, Mr. Medina said, "Okay, you're hired again. Just remember that you were on probation this morning. I'm not paying you for today. I'll start paying you the next time. If you show up."

"Thanks, Mr. Medina. I'll be here."

When I came home, Mom was putting out Bea's breakfast.

I washed my hands in the sink. "Mom," I said. I really wanted to talk to her, tell her about the idea I had for Davi and the letter I was going to write to Grandpa. I was so elated about changing Mr. Medina's mind I knew I could convince Grandpa.

"Mr. Medina fired me, Mom. And then he hired me back!"

"Adam," she interjected, "are you planning on being here this morning for Bea?"

"I'm here. I'm always here in the morning."

"Except when you're not," she said.

"Sorry," I said. "I told you I was sorry."

"I had my hands full yesterday and the day before," she said. "I missed my ride both mornings, and I was late for work, and they're docking my pay."

"Sorry . . . ," I started again, but I cut myself off. Everything I said that started with *sorry* sounded like just a lot of blah-blah-blah. "Don't worry," I said. "I'll take care of Bea."

She picked up her lunch bag and glanced at her watch. "Adam. I'm not taking anything for granted with you anymore."

I opened my mouth and closed it. *Actions*, I told myself. *Actions speak louder than words.*

31

I went down the river path to see if Nancy was around. Woody was there, under a car. "Hi, chief," he said, like he'd seen me yesterday. He stuck a greasy hand out. "Give me that five-eighths-inch wrench there."

I felt like saying, "Get your own wrench." I pushed the whole bunch of greasy tools over and went around to the house to find Nancy. She came out when I called her. She had her hair wound up on top of her head.

"I want to show you something," I said.

"Sure."

We walked up to a place along the bank where there was a bench under a tree. "When did Woody get back?" I asked.

"He's here for the weekend. Did you see that new piece of junk he bought? Do we have to talk about him?"

"Look at this, Nance." I handed her the letter I'd written my grandfather. "Tell me if it's good or not."

She started reading aloud. "'Dear Grandpa.' Good beginning," she said.

Dear Grandpa,

I have a favor to ask you. My best freind, Davi Mori, was with me at Pearl Harbor. Now he and his family are in California, locked up with a lot more Japanese-American families. They didn't do anything, Grandpa. Nothing bad against America, but because of the war the government put them in a place called Manzanar. It's not exactly a prison, but it's not freedom, either.

Davi could leave Manzanar if you said you needed him on the farm. Which I think you do. Davi is strong, and he's smart, and he'd be a good worker for you on the farm, and company, too. I hope you say yes, and write back soon so I can tell Davi.

Your loving grandson,
Adam Pelko

"Do you see any mistakes?" I asked. "I want this letter to be good."

"It's okay," she said. "You need to work on your penmanship. And look here, where you said 'I have a favor to ask'? You're not really asking a favor. It's more like a proposal, right? And you spelled *friend* wrong. *I* before *e*, except after *c*."

"I'll fix it," I said. "Anything else?"

"I like the way you ended it. 'Your loving grandson.' That's very nice."

"Thanks, Nance." She looked so pretty with her hair up, and it was so cute the way she was showing me all the things

I did wrong. "You'll make a great English teacher," I said. "Can I kiss you?"

I didn't know I was going to say that. Then I said it again. "Can I kiss you?"

"Did you ever kiss a girl?"

"Stop acting like a teacher."

"That's the answer. If you had, you'd be crowing about it."

"Okay," I said. "Did you ever kiss a boy?" I really wanted to kiss her now.

"None of your business, junior."

"That means you didn't?"

"It means what it means. It means it's none of your business." She leaned toward me. "This is lesson one. Are you ready, baby?" She put her lips against mine, and we kissed.

32

"Did you hear from your grandfather?" Nancy asked.

"Yes, I got a letter yesterday." I had gone over to the Orange Grove to meet Nancy after work, and we were walking home.

"I haven't heard from Davi yet, but my grandpa wrote, and he said he doesn't care if Davi comes or not, but he wants me to come and live with him. It's not what I expected. So, what do you think of that?"

"What're you going to do? Where is your grandfather, anyway? Is he anywhere near New York City?"

"No, way up north, near Canada. Snow country."

"I don't like snow. Are you going to go?"

"I don't know. My grandfather wants me, and I really like the farm. I learned to milk cows there. My dad wanted me to know everything about the farm. The last time Dad was there, it was haying time. My grandpa drove the wagon. He had both his horses hitched up to the wagon, and I was in back. Dad and the hired man were pitching the raked hay up to me. I was swimming in hay. Scratchy and itchy stuff! And I couldn't stop sneezing."

"It sounds awful."

"No, it was fun. Dragging that big hay wagon into the barn, and then later we had all this food to eat. You work hard and you eat good, and at night the minute your head hits the pillow, you're asleep."

"You really want to do it, don't you? What does your mother say about it?"

"She's not talking to me."

"Two weeks and she's still mad at you?"

I nodded. "Whenever I ask her anything, she says, 'Do what you want, because you'll do it anyway.'"

Nancy patted my head. "I'm sorry. She'll get over it. If you're really thinking about it, you've got to talk to her."

"I know," I said. "I'm just waiting for the right time."

"Bea, what would you say if I went to live with Grandpa?" We were at the playground behind the school, on the seesaw. Bea liked to seesaw with me. She didn't care about the up-and-down part. She just liked being up in the air, sitting there like a little queen.

"Live with Grandpa? No. I won't give you permission."

"Since when do I have to get permission from you?"

"Since forever."

"You can have my room if I go live with Grandpa," I said.

"Don't say those words, Adam. It makes me mad. If you go there, I go and Mommy goes, and we have to write

"Bea." I sat up and let her down slowly. "You know that's not going to happen, don't you?" She looked at me without saying anything, her mouth set. "Come on," I said. "We'll go on the swings now. No more talking."

Dear Adam,

My family had a big powwow about your letter. They were all in on it—Sam, my sister, my parents, of course, even Jesse James had something to say! A bunch of questions. They wanted to know everything. Where would I sleep? How much work would I have to do? What about school? What if your grandfather made me work too much? How did he feel about Japanese people?

The thing is, they know you, but they don't know your grandfather. Also, they don't like the idea of my going so far away from the family. They say it's too dangerous. At least here we're all together.

Listen, don't worry about me. I'm not going to do anything crazy. I just feel that way sometimes, like ten times a day. But whatever happens, it's going to happen to all of us. I guess you could say it's happened already, and like my mom says, we just have to wait it out.

Anyway, thanks, Adam, but you don't have to write to your grandfather for me.

Your friend,
Davi

33

"Let me get this straight," Mom said. She set the iron on end on the ironing board. "You wrote Grandpa and asked if your friend could come live with him. And now he's written back and said what he really wants is for you to come live with him."

"Yes," I said. "Me. He doesn't care about Davi. And anyway, Davi's not going to do it."

"Okay. What are you asking me?"

"What do you think I should tell Grandpa?"

"What do you want to tell him?"

"I don't know. I feel sorry for him all alone."

"He has neighbors, and they all watch out for one another, but if you want to go live with him, Adam, I don't see why you shouldn't. Maybe it's for the best."

"You mean you want me to go?"

She spit on her finger, then touched the iron. It sizzled, and she smoothed out Bea's dress and started ironing again. "Maybe some time away from each other will be good for us both."

Mom put Bea's dress on a hanger and hung it on the doorknob.

Had she heard me? "I'll go," I said again.

She shook out one of my shirts and slipped the sleeve over the ironing board. "You have a lot to do to get ready if you want to get there before school starts," she said.

And just like that, it was decided.

34

I pulled out the big brown suitcase with the leather straps from the back of the attic and threw a couple of things in. And then I pushed the suitcase under the bed and ignored it—except it stuck out a little, and every time I saw it, it said, *You're going. You're going to live with your grandfather.*

But I was still thinking, *What? How did this happen?* It wasn't as if I'd planned it or even been thinking about it. I wrote that letter for Davi so he could get out of Manzanar. But somehow it had turned out that I was the one who was going.

And then I'd think, *Fine! I'm going. Mom wants me to go. Grandpa wants me. Dad would want me to go. I'm going.*

But no matter how many times I said it to myself, it never seemed real.

One morning I was getting dressed, and it was so quiet I could hear Mom and Bea talking downstairs. I couldn't make out what they were saying, but it didn't matter. I stood voice. *Get the train schedule. Write your grandfather. Pack the suitcase. And when are you going to tell Mr. Medina?*

I packed a couple of flannel shirts, then I went out. No reason. It was Sunday. I went down to the river and looked under rocks for salamanders. Every time I picked up a rock, I heard Dad's voice. And then I picked up another rock.

If my father were here, I wouldn't be poking around like this, wasting time. You weren't wishy-washy around him. You didn't say "Yes, I'm going" one minute and "No, I'm not" the next, and you never said "I don't know." He hated that. *Yes or no. Make up your mind.*

I went home, ran up the stairs, emptied my drawers, and threw everything into the suitcase and strapped it shut. I wrote out a tag—ADAM PELKO, C/O OSKAR PELKO, ADAMS CENTER, NEW YORK—and pasted it on the suitcase, then stood it up by the stairs.

There. Done. I was packed. I was going.

In the middle of that night I woke up to my father's voice again. In one ear he was saying, *Go to the farm.* And in the other he was saying, *Stay with your mother.*

I sat up, turned on the light. My room was a mess. Drawers hanging open, clothes and hangers all over the floor. My father would hate it.

I started making the bed the way he'd want it done. I pulled the sheet tight, regulation corners, the blanket tight enough to bounce a coin. I worked fast, the way I used to for his Saturday-morning inspections. Everything off the floor, shoes buffed on my sleeve and lined up, all the hangers in the armoire facing the same way.

I stood at attention at the foot of the bed, the way that pleased him. Back straight, eyes focused, chin tucked in. Waiting for him, waiting for the inspection that was never going to come again.

And I was glad. The thought shot through my mind.

I surveyed the room, the work I'd just done. Good, but not up to my father's standards. My father was foursquare perfect. He was single minded, and I wasn't. I wanted too many different things. I'd never be like him. I'd never be him. I couldn't be him.

And I was glad.

I tore the bed apart, pulled the blanket out, and threw it on the floor. I opened the suitcase, upended it, everything on the floor. When I was done, it looked like a storm, a hurricane, like a tornado, had blown through here. Blown through me.

I got into bed, kicked the sheet free, and lay back on the pillow with my hands behind my head and fell asleep.

35

Dear Grandpa,

I'm sorry I haven't written you sooner. I know you want me to come, and I thought about it a lot, but I can't. Grandpa, I'm sorry, and I know sorry doesn't cut the mustard

I'd written "sorry" three times. I *was* sorry. Every time I thought of him on the farm waiting for me, I was sorry. I put the pen down. What would my dad have said? *Just tell him you made a mistake.*

"Dad, I hear you, but that's not exactly what I want to say."

Dear Grandpa,

I'm not coming to live with you. Grandpa, I love you, and I hate to let you down. I know you want me to come, and I want to, but this isn't the right time. Maybe next year, if you still want me to come.

Love, your grandson,

Adam

PS: I really am sorry.

I mailed the letter on the way to work that morning, and then the whole time on the truck, loading and unloading, stop after stop, I kept saying to myself, *Good, good.*

When I got home, Mom and Mrs. LaValley were outside sitting on the glider. "I hear you're leaving us, Adam," Mrs. LaValley said. "Going far away to help your old grandfather."

Instead of answering, I held up the milk and the pint of sweet cream I'd brought home from the dairy. "I'll put this stuff away, Mom, and then I'm coming back down."

In the kitchen I poured a glass of milk and made a bologna sandwich, and then I paced up and down the room, holding the sandwich. What was I going to say to Mom? *I know you want me to go, and I know I shouldn't change my mind every five minutes . . . okay, I said I'd go, but Mom . . .*

I took a bite of the sandwich, then spit it out in the sink and went downstairs.

Mom was alone. I sat on the railing, facing her. "Mom," I said. And then I pulled out my pay envelope, shook the coins into my hand, and gave her the bills.

"What's this for?" she asked.

"For you."

"I told you I was paying for the train ticket."

"Not the ticket. It's for you, Mom."

"Why?"

"Why?" I said. "I'm working, same as you."

I leaned forward. I knew what I wanted to say. Why didn't I just say it? Why was it so hard for me to say it?

And then I did. I said it. "I'm not going," I said.

"You're yelling," she said, and she was looking at me like Bea did when I said something she didn't understand.

"Mom." I kept my voice steady. "I'm not going to Grandpa's."

"I don't understand."

"Dad . . . ," I began, and then stopped. "Not Dad. Me."

I sat down next to her. "Me! I'm not going to Grandpa's. This is what I want. I mean, what I don't want. I mean, I don't want to leave you and Bea. I'm telling you the truth, Mom. I'd miss you too much. I know you're mad at me, but you won't be mad forever." I sat back. "Okay, Mom?"

"You're not going," she repeated. "Is that your decision?"

"Yes. Are you glad?"

She reached out and took my hand. "Yes, of course I'm glad."

September 15, 1942
Dear Davi,

I got your letter, and I'm glad to hear your father's feeling better. Good news for your family, too, that those other people moved out. Tell your dad I have his mountain stone in my pocket all the time. It's my lucky piece. I think it's already working for me. School's started, and I got every teacher I wanted. How's your school going? You still the smartest kid in the class?

I'm going to teach my friend Nancy to drive. No, she's not my girlfriend. I wish she was. She's got this car her stepfather gave her, one of his old clunkers. It runs, we just have to get gas for it.

Remember what I told you about that guy Babe? I see him around school. He told me his brother who was missing in action turned up wounded in the hospital. I asked him were they going to send his brother home? And this is what he said—I'm quoting: "No, man! They need him. How are they going to win the war without a Gribble?" Same old Babe.

So that's it, that's the big news from Square D Ranch. How about you? What's going on? Any more snake stews? What are you thinking about? I'm still thinking about us signing up together. We have to talk some more about that.

When I have more news, I'll write again. Say hello to your mom and everyone for me, and write me, you dog.

Your friend,

Adam

36

Bea went with me to mail the letter. She was holding my hand and talking nonstop. She had visited the kindergarten she was going to start next week. "We have a sandbox in our class, and a slide. And I told the teacher I know my colors and I can spell my name. I can spell *Mom*. I can spell *Dad*. I told her I can't spell your name yet."

"You don't know how to spell my name? It's easy. *A-D-A-M*."

"*A-D-A-M*." she repeated. "Want me to spell *Dad*? *D-A-D*. I saw Daddy last night."

"You dreamed about him?"

"No, silly! I saw him. He said, 'Hi, Bea.'"

"Did he say anything else?"

"No, but I'll see him again. Does he come and visit you, too?"

"He does." I started to laugh. "He visits me a lot."

"That's very lucky," she said.

"I know, Bea."

At the mailbox Bea insisted on mailing the letter. "I can reach." She got up on her toes, but she couldn't quite make it, and I lifted her up. She dropped the letter into the slot. Then we walked home together.

Pacific War—1942

Two weeks after Pearl Harbor was attacked on December 7, 1941, 43,000 troops of the Japanese Fourteenth Army landed on the Philippine mainland. Despite overwhelming force, and without supplies, relief, or an effective air force, the Allied forces under Gen. Douglas MacArthur resisted for nearly six months.

January 2: Manila falls to the Japanese.

January 5: U.S. and Filipino troops retreat to Bataan. Military rations are cut in half.

January 15: Japan advances into Burma.

January 30: British troops retreat into Singapore.

February 15: British troops in Singapore surrender to the Japanese army.

February 19: Japanese carrier-based planes bomb Darwin, Australia, in the largest Japanese air attack since Pearl Har-

MacArthur to leave the island fortress of Corregidor in the Philippines and take command of the Australian defense.

February 23: A Japanese submarine surfaces and bombards the U.S. coast at Santa Barbara, California.

February 27: The carrier USS *Langley,* carrying crated planes desperately needed for the defense of Australia, is sunk by the Japanese.

February 27–March 1: The Battle of Java Sea ends in Japanese victory.

March 4: American admiral "Bull" Halsey, in a bold, symbolic gesture, attacks Marcus Island, less than one thousand miles from Japan.

March 11: General MacArthur escapes Corregidor and takes command of Allied forces in Australia.

April 6: First U.S. troops land in Australia.

April 9: U.S. and Filipino troops surrender in Bataan. The Bataan Death March, which follows, takes the lives of thousands of Filipino and American troops.

April 18: Lt. Col. Jimmy Doolittle leads an attack of sixteen B-25s against the Japanese mainland. Japan has never been bombed before. Only one American plane returns.

May 6: In the last message from Corregidor before it fell, Gen. Jonathan M. Wainwright reports, "With broken heart and with head bowed in sadness, but not in shame . . . today

I must arrange terms for the surrender of the fortified islands of Manila Bay."

May 7: The Battle of the Coral Sea begins, in which Japanese landing forces aimed at Port Moresby, near Australia, are turned back. This is the first all-carrier naval battle of the war, a battle in which the opposing ships, relying solely on air power, never sight their opponents.

May 20: Japanese forces capture Burma and reach the border of India.

May: Japan assembles an armada of more than two hundred ships, including eleven battleships, eight aircraft carriers, plus cruisers, destroyers, and submarines. The plan is for a force of 5,000 veteran Japanese soldiers to wade ashore at Midway Island and take control of the huge American naval base. But the Americans have broken the Japanese code and are prepared for the attack with 3,600 troops on the island, but only three aircraft carriers to the Japanese's eight.

June 4–5: In the early stages of the naval battle at Midway the Japanese planes—which are more numerous, faster, and more maneuverable than the American counterparts—destroy planes, hangars, and buildings. After three waves of attack the Americans have lost thirty-five of forty-one attack planes and failed to hit a single enemy ship. Then, in six

American attack bombers sink three Japanese air-

June 21: A Japanese submarine again shells the American coast near the mouth of the Columbia River, more a symbolic attack than a real one.

August 7: The United States First Marine Division, under Lt. Gen. Alexander Vandegrift, lands 10,000 troops on Guadalcanal to no opposition. An almost completed airfield was taken easily.

September 9: A Japanese submarine launches a float plane off the Oregon coast that drops incendiary bombs near Brookings, Oregon, the only aerial bombing of the United States during World War II.

November 13: In naval clashes off Guadalcanal the five Sullivan brothers, all serving on the cruiser *Juneau* are killed in action.

December: Italian physicist Enrico Fermi and a team of European and American scientists achieve the first nuclear chain reaction at the University of Chicago.

December 31: After six months of fighting, the defeated Japanese evacuate Guadalcanal. American forces have suffered 2,000 dead and 20,000 wounded. The Japanese have suffered 30,000 casualties.

Home Front—1942

After Pearl Harbor a wave of revulsion and hatred swept indiscriminately over the Japanese-American population, citizens or not. On February 19, 1942, President Franklin Delano Roosevelt issued Executive Order 9066, authorizing the military to designate restricted zones from which "any and all persons might be excluded." Though they were not specifically named, this order was aimed at the Japanese-American population on the West Coast.

On April 1, 1942, the army began the forced evacuation and internment of all Japanese Americans living in the Pacific Coast states. Lt. Gen. J. L. DeWitt stated publicly and without disapproval, "A Jap's a Jap. It makes no difference whether he's an American or not." More than 5,000 Japanese Americans were confined at the Fresno Assembly Center. Ultimately, 112,000 Americans of Japanese descent, 70,000 of whom were United States citizens, were confined for up to four years in ten camps in desolate areas of Califor the draft. Fifty million men registered, and sixteen million men aged eighteen to thirty-six were drafted. President Roosevelt proudly carried his draft card until the end of the war.

Women did not have to register, but 300,000 volunteered for military service, despite the prejudice of the times, which viewed military women disparagingly and put them at risk for harassment. The prejudice women endured, however, paled compared with the treatment of nearly one million African-American servicemen.

The War Price and Rationing Board was created to distribute limited supplies equally. Food rationing began with coffee and sugar. To save gas, the speed limit was cut to 35 mph. Cars carried color-coded letters, designating how much gas the driver was entitled to. The letter *A*, for example, entitled the car to three to five gallons a week.

In June, President Roosevelt called on the public to turn in "old tires, old rubber raincoats, old garden hoses, rubber shoes, bathing caps, gloves."

With sixteen million men in the armed forces, the civilian labor force was made up of groups previously excluded: women, blacks, the handicapped, the old, and the young. Six million women, few of whom had been employed before, took jobs during the war in factories, at shipyards, in steel mills, and on the railroads. Three million adolescents, some as young as twelve, were also employed. This labor force of the excluded armed the Allied armies with the guns, munitions, ships, planes, trucks, and cars needed to defeat Japan, Germany, and their allies. It was the most productive labor force in American history.

Historical
Documents

Due Notice. Dated April 1, 1942, this notice appeared in poster form all over California and was no April Fool's joke. It led to a serious and tragic disruption of the lives of many thousands of people.

WESTERN DEFENSE COMMAND
AND FOURTH ARMY
WARTIME CIVIL CONTROL ADMINISTRATION
Presidio of San Francisco, California
April 1, 1942
INSTRUCTIONS
TO ALL PERSONS OF
JAPANESE ANCESTRY

Living in the Following Area:

All that portion of the City and County of San Francisco, State of California, lying generally west of the north-south line established by Junipero Serra Boulevard, Worchester Avenue, and Nineteenth Avenue, and lying generally north of the east-west line established by California Street, to the intersection of Market Street, and thence on Market Street to San Francisco Bay.

All Japanese persons, both alien and non-alien, will be evacuated from the above designated area by 12:00 o'clock noon Tuesday, April 7, 1942.

No Japanese person will be permitted to enter or leave the above described area after 8:00 a.m., Thursday, April 2, 1942, without obtaining special permission from the Provost Marshal at the Civil Control Station located at:

> 1701 Van Ness Avenue
> San Francisco, California

On Feb. 19, 1942, President Franklin Delano Roosevelt signed executive order 9066 authorizing the exclusions of over 120,000 persons of Japanese ancestry, 2/3 of whom were American citizens. They were uprooted from their West Coast homes and moved by the United States Government to . . . temporary quarters at race tracks and fairgrounds, then to detention camps in desolate areas of the United States. The average period of incarceration was three years. . . . None were ever charged with any act of disloyalty. . . . This memorial is dedicated to the individuals and their struggle to overcome this tragic violation of civil rights. May such injustice and humiliation never recur.

—FROM A MEMORIAL PLAQUE AT THE
FRESNO COUNTY FAIRGROUNDS

May the injustices and humiliation suffered here as a result of hysteria, racism and economic exploitation never emerge again.

On February 19, 1976, on the thirty-fourth anniversary of Executive Order 9066, President Gerald Ford issued a proclamation officially declaring "February 19 is the anniversary of a sad day in American history. . . . [A]nd we now know what we should have known then—not only was the evacuation wrong, but Japanese Americans were and are loyal Americans."

On August 10, 1988, President Ronald Reagan signed the Civil Liberties Act which authorized the payment of $20,000 to each eligible person of Japanese ancestry who had been confined, held in custody, relocated, or otherwise deprived of liberty or property as a result of Executive Order 9066.

In 1990, President George Bush accompanied the payments with a letter, which said in part, "A monetary sum and words alone can not restore lost years or erase painful memories: neither can they fully convey our Nation's resolve to rectify injustice and to uphold the rights of individuals. We can never fully right the wrongs of the past, but we can take a clear stand for justice and recognize that serious injustices were done to Japanese Americans during World War II."

On February 19, 1992, a bill passed both houses of Congress declaring the former internment camp, Manzanar, as a National Historic Site.

Literature Circle Questions

Use these questions and the activities that follow to get more out of the experience of reading *A Boy No More* by Harry Mazer.

1. Where was Adam during the attack on Pearl Harbor? What was he doing at the time? Who was with him?

2. What does Davi ask Adam to deliver to his father? According to Davi, why is it important that Mr. Mori receive this item?

3. What lie does Adam tell Jerry while they are on the train?

4. Why doesn't Adam like his new home in San Diego?

5. What do Adam and Babe Gribble have in common? How does Babe's attitude toward Adam change over the course of the story?

6. Which character in the story has aspirations of becoming an English teacher? Do you think this character will make a good English teacher? Explain your answer using details from the text.

7. Choose one character who helps Adam on his journey from Bakersfield to Manzanar. Imagine you are that character and give a brief description of Adam. What does he look like? What is Adam wearing? Based on what Adam has told you, why do you think he is going to Manzanar?

8. Think back to Adam's first day of school in Bakersfield. Imagine you are in Adam's class. What would you say to him to make him feel welcome? What would you ask him about his experiences?

9. Why do you think Adam decided not to go to New York State to live with Grandpa Pelko? Do you support his decision? What would you have done if you were Adam?

10. What does Mr. Mori give Adam? What does this gift symbolize? Why do you think this gift was so important to Adam?

11. Describe the scene at the Hotel Royale in chapter 17. Who does Adam speak to at the hotel? Based on what you learned in the story and in the author's note at the end of the book, what do you think had happened in Chinatown since the attack on Pearl Harbor?

12. Choose one female character from the story and one male character from the story. Compare and contrast each character's contribution to the war effort. What contribution would you have made to the war effort?

13. Re-read the author's description of the home front on pages 131–132. Choose a historical event or fact described by the author and explain how that event or fact plays a part in the story you just read.

14. In chapter 11, Mr. Ewing announces to the class that "we have a hero in our midst." Who does Mr. Ewing think is a hero? Do you agree with Mr. Ewing? Why or why not?

15. Now that you have read the story, consider the title of the book. Why do you think the author chose this title for his book? Do you think it was a good choice? Use evidence from the text to support your argument.

Note: These questions are keyed to Bloom's Taxonomy as follows: Knowledge: 1–3; Comprehension: 4–5; Application: 6–8; Analysis: 9–11; Synthesis: 12–13; Evaluation: 14–15

Activities

1. Draw a map of California from Fresno to San Diego. Add other key towns from the story you can remember, including Bakersfield and Oakland. Be sure to include other points like Manzanar and Mt. Whitney. Then, trace Adam's journey to Fresno and his journey to Manzanar. Create a legend with symbols beside your map to show what Adam did or how he felt in each place. For example, you may want to use a fork or plate to show each location where you remember that Adam ate a meal or felt hungry.

2. Imagine you are Adam and you decide to enter an essay contest. The only rule of the contest is that the essay should be about someone you admire. If you were Adam, whom would you choose? What would you say about this person? List two or three things you admire about this person and describe why you admire this person in those ways.

3. Create a title acrostic. Write the title of the book down the side of a piece of paper with one letter per line, one on top of another. For each letter in the title, write a sentence that begins with that letter and tells something significant about the story. For example, after N you might write, "Nancy worked at the restaurant where Adam and his family ate dinner."

Other Books by This Author:
A Boy at War: A Novel of Pearl Harbor, Aladdin Library (November 2002)
The Wild Kid, Aladdin Library (July 2001)
The Last Mission, Laurel Leaf (January 1981)